Ménage on Moone Mountain

THE MEN OF MOONE MOUNTAIN BOOK ONE

BELLA SETTARRA

~ *Acknowledgements* ~

I would like to acknowledge the help of Mary Yakovets, who pointed me in the right direction when I needed to do research for this series. Thank you for your help, Mary. Your guidance and friendship are invaluable. ☺

Copyright

Second print publication: May 2022 – Bella Settarra Publishing

Chapter One

Deputy Freeman pulled his dusty SUV into the garage outside the Freemont Ranch house and sighed. He grabbed his hat from the passenger seat, and slammed the car door with the finality of a kid at the beginning of summer break.

Travis Beaumont strode toward him, his shirtsleeves rolled up to his bulging biceps and mud on his chin. "There's a storm brewing!"

"Not my problem. I'll be holed up in front of that fire with a whiskey by the time the heavens open." The deputy looked at the blackening sky, shook his fair head, and headed for the house.

Travis sniggered. He knew his partner was tired after a couple of particularly grueling weeks on the job and was glad he had decided to take some time off. Although he still had the ranch to run, he was looking forward to having Kent Freeman around for a while.

A sudden flash of lightning lit up the whole of Moone Mountain, and Travis stopped in his tracks. He had intended to go inside and greet his boyfriend properly but thought better of it. The horses might have been spooked by the weather.

He hadn't reached the stables before he heard the loud thudding of hooves. He recognized the black horse that shot out of the forest to the side of the ranch. Blackie was one of the stable owner's best. And he was wearing a saddle.

"Kent, get out here!" Travis ran over to the skittish horse, slowing his pace as he neared him. He spoke softly to the large beast, which reared slightly and then calmed a little. Travis grabbed hold of the reins and patted its sweaty flank.

He walked the horse to the stable.

"What's up?" Kent had evidently already stripped for his shower and stood on the front porch in nothing but a small towel loosely wrapped around his waist. Travis's mouth watered at the sight as he walked past. Kent's hair looked golden in the evening sun, and his herculean chest rippled as he leaned over the balustrade. His big, green eyes twinkled, despite his tiredness, and his perfect teeth gleamed in his handsome, tanned face. He must have caught the look Travis gave him, because he grinned salaciously.

"Blackie just came out of the forest," Travis called over to him. "He's saddled up. Wanna call to see if he's lost a rider?"

The deputy didn't need asking twice. He shot back inside the house to call the owner of the local riding stables, Fred Hammond.

Travis had settled Blackie in the stall and saddled his own horse, Mustard, by the time Kent came out with the news. "There was a young girl, Caucasian, mid-twenties, name's Brooke Adams. A competent rider, Fred reckons, so he let her take Blackie out for a couple of hours."

"Brooke Adams? I don't know the name." Travis frowned. He and Kent knew the names of everyone in Moone County, especially the women.

"You need me to come?" Kent was still wrapped in the towel, looking up at the cowboy mounted up and ready to go.

"No, you stay here in case she shows up. I'll take a look around." Travis winked at his partner as he rode Mustard toward the forest.

A roar of thunder warned him it wouldn't be long before the inevitable deluge. Mustard slowed down when they reached the edge of the dark woodland, and they made for the track most of Fred's riders used. It was unusual for him to let someone take one of his horses unaccompanied, so this girl must be a really good rider. Plus, Blackie was a powerful beast. Fred wouldn't let a real beginner ride him.

As they ventured deeper into the undergrowth, it got harder to see. Travis knocked his hat up his forehead to peer around the trees. Up ahead the path rose steeply, leaving a deep ravine to either side. He frowned, hoping that wasn't where the horse had lost his rider. It would be just his luck to be sliding down there when the rain started to fall. *Fuck!* If it wasn't for bad luck, this cowboy would have no luck at all.

He saw something blue about halfway down the incline. He stopped Mustard on the muddy track, slipped off and went to inspect the situation, just as it got even worse. The rain started. *Great.*

He could just make out a mass of blonde hair on the girl who lay next to a rock partway down the gully. It wasn't too steep, so he took the chance and began to climb down. Big spots of rain pelted him like bullets, mocking his efforts. He gritted his teeth. If he could get to her before it became too sodden, he'd have a good chance of getting them both back up. His foot slid on some loose rock, and he cursed. He had to remove his gloves to get a good grip on the boulders on the way down the valley, but he eventually reached the spot where the girl in blue jeans and a once-white shirt lay sprawled face down in the mud.

"Can you hear me, darlin'?" He carefully held her face and winced at the amount of blood that poured from a wound on her forehead. The rock had broken her fall, but at what cost? She was totally unresponsive. He quickly checked her out for broken bones before hoisting her up in his muscular arms. She was a soft handful and very comfortable to hold on to.

Travis shook his head as the rain dripped off his hat, and attempted the climb back up. He'd grown up around here, and was well-used to scrabbling about in the mud. It was a little harder with a full-grown woman in your arms, though. He grappled at the roots that wound around some of the boulders, and used the rocks for support as he fought against the driving rain to reach the track at the top of the ravine.

"Good boy, Mustard," he soothed his horse before hoisting himself and the sleeping beauty into the saddle. Holding her tight in one arm, he used the other to steer the reins. Mustard went steadily along the muddy paths and down the track. The storm rumbled on, and the rain assaulted them as they fought their way home.

"I was getting worried." Kent was waiting for them when they arrived at the stable. He'd evidently managed a quick wash and put on some fresh jeans. He looked gorgeous. He'd already tended to Blackie. He took the girl from Travis's arms, enabling the cowboy to easily slide out of the saddle and tend his horse before following them inside.

"The storm's getting worse," Travis said as they made it to the front door. "I found her partway down the ravine. Looks like she hit her head on the rock which stopped her fall."

"We won't get the doc out in this weather." Kent frowned as he carried her down the corridor that led to the bedrooms. It was a large house, originally built for a family. Now that the boys lived there, it had a few alterations. A different type of playroom, for one. Kent carried her into a large bedroom at the bottom of the hallway. He frowned as he looked at the white bedspread, then back at the heap of mud in his arms.

"Can we take her clothes off?" Travis asked doubtfully.

"I think we'll have to. She's soaked through. We can't put her to bed like this."

While Kent continued to hold her, Travis first removed her muddy Justin Ropers, then her soaking-wet socks. He prayed she wouldn't wake up to find him removing her jeans. His hands shook as he undid her shirt. She stirred slightly in Kent's arms and Travis froze.

"Leave it on for now," Kent whispered, obviously not wanting to disturb or frighten the poor girl.

Travis placed a towel on the pillow before Kent laid her down in the fluffy, white bed. With a soft, wet cloth, Travis wiped the mess from her face. He smiled as he revealed a very attractive young girl.

"That's quite a deep gash," Kent remarked as he reappeared with the first aid kit. Travis dabbed the wound with some soft gauze. Kent handed over a large dressing, and Travis soon had it covered.

"You've got to admit she's real pretty." Travis smiled.

"Forget it, bro."

"You don't know," Travis retaliated with a frown.

"She's either spoken for or she wouldn't be interested in what we're offering."

"I don't see a ring." Travis smirked.

"That don't mean a thing." Kent left to return the first aid kit.

His partner sighed. Kent had really liked Kathy. He hadn't let anyone new get close to him for more than a night or two since she left.

Travis dimmed the lights, leaving the room in a yellowish glow. The walls were painted a pale primrose, and the floral curtains enclosed the bedroom in a warm radiance. The storm continued to rage outside the window, but the house was snug and warm.

"I'll sit with her awhile," Travis called.

He thought he heard a reply from Kent, who sounded as though he was down the hall. Settling in the chair beside the bed, Travis sighed and closed his eyes.

A few minutes later, Kent was back. "I've put a pie in the oven."

"Thanks, Mom." He opened his eyes, grinning mischievously.

Kent snorted. "And you'd better get out of those wet things." His voice was deep and masterful.

Travis chuckled. "You offering to help with that?" He cocked an eyebrow at his partner.

"Hell, yeah." Kent took Travis's arm and hauled him out of the room. They left the door open just in case Brooke should wake, and headed down the hall to another large bedroom.

Travis's dark, tousled hair dripped over his muscular shoulders as Kent led him into the room. Their room. It was painted in pale green and had checkered curtains. The bedspread was a pale eau de nil green and stretched endlessly across the oversized bed.

Kent had hold of Travis's belt buckle as he pulled him closer. "Not only do you have too many clothes on for my liking, but you'll catch your death in these," he growled.

Travis said nothing, just raised an eyebrow expectantly. Kent licked his lips as he admired the way Travis's wet shirt outlined his taut eight-pack. His fingers trembled as he slowly unfastened the buttons of the checkered cotton.

Travis's deep-brown eyes grew darker as Kent gazed into them adoringly. Kent smirked appreciatively at his partner's wet body while he peeled the shirt over the cowboy's huge biceps and threw it carelessly onto the floor. He gasped at the delectable sight of his partner's ripped, slightly hairy chest. He couldn't resist the urge to suck a cold, hard nipple into his hot, wet mouth and was rewarded with a deep moan.

Kent stroked Travis's hard chest, sinking slowly down his perfect abs toward the teasing dark hairs that heralded the start of his happy trail. He caught Travis's gaze and made short work of the cowboy's buckle and fly. Travis had already heeled off his boots by the time Kent scraped off the soaking wet jeans which clung enticingly to Travis's huge thighs. As usual, Travis had gone commando, and his massive member sprang free.

Kent afforded himself a quick glance at the thick

cock he loved so much, and grinned to see its head already glistening with anticipation. His strong hand grabbed the shaft and he heard Travis exhale sharply as he began stroking it gently.

Travis's hands flew to Kent's fly and soon divested him of his jeans. Kent had also dispensed with underwear tonight, and his cock stood proudly at attention, already glistening with excitement. He gasped as Travis closed his fingers around his cock, and their hands entwined as they rubbed both dicks together, finding their rhythm as they panted with desire.

"Kiss me, bud." Travis's voice was a raspy growl.

Kent grazed his lips across his lover's and Travis closed his eyes. Kent nibbled his way along his mouth before demanding entry. Travis's thick tongue came to welcome him in and both tongues tangled erratically as passion enveloped both men.

The air was thick with their panting and moaning as their heat rose and their bodies meshed together. Travis suddenly spun him around and backed him onto the vast bed. Kent looked up as the cowboy's massive body towered over him as they continued to rub their rock-hard cocks together. Pre-cum oozed over their hands, enabling them to glide effortlessly over each other.

"I want you, bro." Kent heard the huskiness in his own voice and sensed his pleading eyes were glazing over. With one hand on Travis's cock and another grabbing his hair, he yanked the cowboy's mouth to his and desperately sought his tongue.

Travis returned the kiss as he pushed Kent's quivering knees up to meet his chest. The position caused Kent to rock back slightly, opening himself up. Travis worked the creamy pre-cum down Kent's soft perineum to lubricate his asshole. He used his thick finger to probe and tantalize his lover's rim. Instinctively, Kent tensed up at the intrusion.

"Shh, relax, bud," Travis soothed into his mouth.

Kent let out a deep breath slowly. Travis must have felt his ass unclench, and he murmured his approval. The cowboy's finger slid into the tight hole as Kent hissed sharply.

"Shh." Travis continued to sooth him as he pressed his finger in harder, breaking through the tight rim of muscle, and slowly maneuvered in and out of his ass. Kent adjusted and started to relax, and his partner took the opportunity to slide another finger in. Pain momentarily seared through his body before morphing into exquisite pleasure. Travis continued his loving assault on his over sensitized ass as he stroked the cowboy's other hand, and they entangled lovingly, still rubbing their thick cocks against each other.

"I'm nearly there," Kent gasped.

"Hold on, bud." Travis glided his massive cock down and nudged at Kent's ass. With one big thrust he forced it inside, causing both men to hiss like feral cats.

Kent reached up his big hands and clung to Travis's thick, hard biceps. Travis grabbed Kent's hip and continued to stroke his partner's engorged cock in time to his heaving thrusts into his tight ass.

Kent stared up into his lover's dark eyes and marveled at the desire he found staring back at him. "I love you, bro," Kent admitted in a breathy sigh.

Travis grinned, looking slightly surprised. Kent guessed it was because he didn't usually give way to bouts of sentiment. "I love you too, buddy," he assured him before switching up a gear. Travis hammered hard into his ass, and Kent couldn't help the grunts that escaped him as he gasped for breath. The thrusts continued to increase as Travis pulled harder on Kent's throbbing cock with his fist.

"I'm gonna blow!" Kent gasped.

"Me, too, bud, right into this hot little ass of yours," Travis promised.

The heat of his words caused Kent to erupt, shooting his load up over his stomach. "Yes, yes!" he shouted as stars flashed in front of his eyes.

"Yessss!" Travis grunted as he shot his hot seed into his panting lover.

Travis slumped onto the bed next to the deputy, both smiling and gasping for air as they shivered with aftershocks.

A woman's screams pulled the men from their reverie, and they both leapt to their feet, yanked on their Levis, and ran down the hall, still panting hard.

The young blonde was sitting up in bed, clutching the cover and staring into the space in front of her.

"It's OK, baby, no one's gonna hurt you. You're safe." Kent's voice was soft and low as he put an arm around her shoulder. At the sound of his voice, she suddenly stopped staring and flitted her eyes nervously, first at him, then the room, then Travis. The cowboy stood in the doorway, watching patiently. He evidently loved the look of the beautiful woman in his lover's arms.

Kent was cooing and shushing her while stroking her back with his big hand. She seemed to relax a little.

"That's it, baby," he soothed. "It's all right. My name's Kent and this here's Travis. We've brought you to the Freemont Ranch. You fell down the ravine in the storm. Do you remember?"

She nodded, her wet, muddy hair shaking around her soft, round face. "The horse got spooked by something and he bolted. I remember my hand slipping from the reins. I couldn't hold on." She was starting to panic. Kent nodded for Travis to wrap her shoulders in the blanket.

"It's all right now, darlin'," Travis told her softly. "I've stabled Blackie for the night and told Fred where you are. Is there anyone else we need to tell?"

She shook her head sadly.

"You're not from around here, are you, baby?" Kent rubbed her hair with a towel. It resulted in a rather muddy towel, but at least he managed to get some of the cold water from her hair.

She shook her head again. "My name's Brooke... Adams. I'm just taking a short vacation."

"What on earth brought you to Moone County,

darlin'? There's nothing here and it's not exactly high season." Travis was just being curious, but Kent could see that she looked a little hurt.

"It's very beautiful. And quiet." Her voice was soft and a little sad.

"The Moone Falls are lovely, and it certainly is peaceful. Did you just want a relaxing break?" Kent tried to cajole her a little.

She nodded, and then sniffed.

"We'd best get you out of those wet things before you catch your death of cold." Travis must be too concerned about her shivering to worry about answers to their questions. Enough of the good cop, bad cop for now. Kent watched as he strolled through the archway that led to the en-suite bathroom and switched on the shower. It heated almost immediately, and hot steam started to fill the room. He heard his partner go to a wall cabinet and pull out some bottles, which he must have then placed on the glass shelf inside the shower.

"You can take a bath if you prefer, Brooke. Kent offered as Travis returned to the bedroom, his bare chest dripping wet. He smirked as Travis rolled his eyes.

Brooke must have caught their expressions and giggled. It was a lovely sound; like the jingle of little bells, almost musical. Both men smiled at her. She slid out of bed, wrapping the blanket around her. "A shower would be lovely, thank you," she assured them.

"I'll wait in here in case you need anything. I don't

want you collapsing on us with that head wound," Travis insisted.

"I'll be fine, honestly." She looked a little shocked at his suggestion.

"Travis is right, baby. You could keel over at any time. Pity we can't get Doc Hardy up here to take a look at you, but he'd never get up the mountain in this weather, especially as it's dark out there."

Brooke pouted. "OK. But you will stay in here, won't you?"

"You have my word as a gentleman," Kent promised with a smile.

"There's towels on the rack all ready for you," Travis informed her as she stepped shyly through the archway.

"I'll grab her something to wear." Kent turned as he reached the door. "Don't you forget what I said about being a gentleman, now will you?"

"I won't forget you said *you'd* be one." Travis wore a salacious grin.

"I was talking for the both of us. Don't you dare take one foot in there; you'll likely frighten her to death!" Kent gave Travis his *I'm warning you* look.

"Don't worry. I won't go into the bathroom. Looks like it wouldn't take much, anyhow, poor thing." Travis held his hands up in submission. His dark brown eyes twinkled in mirth.

Satisfied, Kent left the room.

～

Travis opened the bedroom window to let some of the steam escape. In doing so, he realized he had managed to angle himself so he could just see Brooke's reflection in the mirror of the closet door, which he had accidentally left open. Screwing his eyes shut to protect her modesty, he felt a burn in his stomach. He longed to open his eyes just for a second. He bit his lip as the yearning overpowered him. Eventually he allowed himself a tiny peek with just one eye. It wasn't enough. Both eyes suddenly opened wide and he grinned.

The glass of the shower cubicle was completely transparent, and he could see her face smiling up as the water streamed down on her. The steam was starting to dissipate, and he could just see her large, full bosom.

She turned slightly so her back was toward him. His immediate disappointment was replaced with horror. Large welts covered her whole back and her beautiful, round ass. They continued down to the tops of her legs. He gauged that a single tail had been used in the hands of some maniac who didn't have a clue how to handle it. Scars crisscrossed haphazardly across her soft, pale flesh, with some newer, almost-open cuts over her skin. He averted his eyes quickly and moved back toward the bed as he heard the water being turned off.

"I thought she could sleep in one of your old shirts tonight, and there's some of my old clothes for tomorrow. Think that'll be OK?" Kent burst through the bedroom door and placed a pile of clothes on the ottoman.

Travis nodded. Kent must have caught his expression before he could hide it. A slight shake of Travis's head told him the explanation would have to wait, as Brooke entered the room, smiling. One large towel was wrapped around her body, with a smaller one covering her shoulders.

And the scars.

Chapter Two

The sun was shining when Brooke awoke in the large, soft bed the next morning. She sighed, remembering where she was. Her head ached and she could feel bruises throbbing all over her body, but it was nothing compared to what she was used to. She bit her lip and crawled out of bed. If she was quick and quiet enough, she might just be able to leave before the two men got up. Although she liked the handsome strangers very much, and was grateful for their kindness, she didn't want to answer the myriad questions that would certainly be waiting for her, especially after last night.

They had enjoyed a lovely meat and vegetable pie, which Kent had cooked for them and sat talking for a while before she went to bed. Well, *they* had sat talking. She had spent most of the evening asking them questions to avoid answering too many of theirs.

She had told them she was a keen rider and that she was staying at the Montgomery Hotel in town. They knew she was on vacation and had come for some peace and quiet. Nothing they couldn't have checked out for themselves if they'd had a mind to. She had evaded the issue of where she came from by simply telling them she was a city girl, and they seemed content with her employment as just "admin."

"Morning, beautiful." She had only gotten one foot out of the bedroom door when Travis walked up the hall wearing nothing but a towel and Giorgio Armani.

She gasped. He looked as gorgeous as he smelled. Water was still running from his tousled hair down his ripped, slightly hairy chest, and his stubble was neatly groomed. His dark brown eyes twinkled, and he had an amazing smile.

"Good morning," she replied. She actually felt far from beautiful in big, baggy jeans, a large shirt, and a pair of sneakers that were a couple of sizes too big for her, but she was grateful to have clean, dry clothes. Her only worry was not having any underwear on, and her breasts were a little too large to go without a bra. Her nipples hardened as his gaze swept over her, and she was sure he could see them through the shirt. She folded her arms to try to hide her embarrassment—and arousal.

"Kent's got breakfast on. I'll be there in a minute." Travis's smile seemed to have broadened, and she flushed as he turned and went back to his room.

She could smell pancakes as soon as she neared the kitchen, and her stomach rumbled in anticipation.

"I don't eat breakfast, thank you," she lied as Kent placed a plateful on the table.

"You do now, baby." He obviously wasn't about to argue with her. He nodded to a chair in front of her expectantly.

Brooke flushed. He wasn't asking her, he was *telling* her. There was evidently no question in his mind that she wouldn't comply.

She felt a little nervous as she sat down. He was another gorgeous guy. He wore a plaid, short-sleeved shirt and Levis, which framed his pert ass beautifully. He had lovely blond, curly hair, which kissed the top of his collar, and his muscles rippled in his arms as he moved competently around the kitchen.

Her stomach growled again and he gave a satisfied smirk. *Damn!*

"Storm's finished. There's a couple of trees down toward the foot of the mountain, but it's mostly passable now." Travis breezed in and took the seat next to her. He was dressed in jeans and cotton checkered shirt and smelled divine. His buttons were mainly undone, allowing a little of his chest hair to peep through enticingly. Brooke was suddenly aware that she was staring at his chest, licking her lips. Judging by the twinkle in his eyes, Travis must have been aware too. She caught his gaze and flushed.

"That's good. I think we might call Doc Hardy out to take a look at our girl in that case," Kent announced and took a bite of his breakfast.

Brooke flushed. "I'm fine. I need to get back, anyhow," she said, a little flustered as she took a sip of her coffee. Somehow she had to stay focused.

"Back where, darlin'?" Travis looked surprised.

"I need to get Blackie back to Mr. Hammond, and then I need to go to the hotel and let them know I'm still here. They might think I've left without paying or something."

"Well now, I just came from dropping Blackie off at Fred Hammond's place this morning, and Kent informed the hotel last night that you were here. Don Montgomery was very grateful too. Seems he got a little worried when you didn't get back before the storm." Travis reached across for the sugar, giving Brooke another waft of his masculine scent as he did so. God, he smelled good.

Brooke bit her lip in frustration before biting into the pancakes. She couldn't help but obey Kent's order.

"How long are you planning to stay in Moone?" Kent asked. He finished up his food.

"Um, I'm not sure yet."

"Well, how about I go into town and fetch your things from the hotel and you can stay here for a bit? You really shouldn't be on your own, and you obviously like horses. I'm sure we could use an extra pair of hands around here for a while if you want to make yourself useful, and we can show you the local sights. Can't be much fun on your own." Kent seemed to have it all sorted out.

Travis grinned at her.

"That's very kind of you, but I can't, really. I hardly know you and I'd only be in your way. Besides, I really like my own company. I'm quite happy exploring on my own." Brooke tried to sound light and cheerful, but they just stared at her.

"Don't you like us?" Travis's gorgeous face fell as he spoke, and she longed to put her hands either side of it and pull it into a long kiss. Her cheeks warmed at the idea. She never had thoughts like that.

"No...I mean, it's not that. Of course I like you. I'm really grateful for all your help. It's just..." She didn't even know what she was trying to say.

"Just what?" Kent got to his feet and took his dishes to the sink. Brooke jumped up and lifted her plate to do the same. The room started to spin and colors seemed to melt into each other. The pain in her head got worse, and she was vaguely aware of muffled voices and then Travis's strong arms enveloping her.

Confusion filled Brooke's mind. Muted voices surrounded her, and she felt as if she were floating. She was no longer wrapped in the security of Travis's strong arms, and the thought made her feel strangely bereft.

"She's coming back around now. Expect her to be

groggy for a few days, but she should be OK. I'll leave you some painkillers. They should help but might make her a bit sleepy, so go easy." An old man's voice came into Brooke's world as she slowly opened her eyes.

The sunlight was almost too bright, and she winced. She was lying on the sofa she had sat on last night. A strange man was peering over her, and she could smell Travis's lovely scent. She tried to sit up, looking around for him, but the old man stopped her.

"Now don't you move, missy. You need some rest, d'ya hear?"

She frowned at him.

She heard a chuckle that she recognized as Travis, and was relieved when he came into her line of vision. Everything was still slightly blurry, and the sounds of the men's voices seemed to be somewhere in the distance. Travis crouched at the side of the sofa as the man stood up. "It's all right, darlin'."

She found that gorgeous, deep voice very reassuring and immediately began to relax as he took her hand. His palm felt rough and slightly calloused, and seemed to swamp hers. She suddenly felt safer than she had in a long time.

"Call me if you need me again, but I reckon she'll be fine now." The old man was putting on his hat. "I'll see myself out."

"Thanks, Doc," Travis called after him without taking his warm eyes off Brooke.

The room had finally come back into focus, and she

watched the door close behind the old man. She looked back to Travis gazing down at her.

"Looks like you're stuck with us for a while," he informed her with a smile. "Doc Hardy's orders. We need to keep a close eye on you for a couple of days. Think you can handle that?"

For the first time in ages, Brooke felt her pussy clench. The thought of these two handsome hunks looking after her for the next few days both excited and frightened her. She dropped her gaze in embarrassment, only to hear that low chuckle again. He seemed to read her thoughts.

"Where's Kent?" She suddenly noticed they were alone.

"In town. He's gone to pick up a few supplies and get your things while he's there. No point in you paying the hotel while you're staying here." Travis's lazy drawl was so matter-of-fact, she almost accepted what he said without thinking. Almost.

"Hang on. I-I can't stay here," she stammered as she sat up.

"Well, we can't look after you while you're in town and we're up here, now can we?" He sounded incredulous, as if there was no question she would do as he planned.

Brooke's mind raced. She couldn't move in with two guys she'd only just met.

"Hey, it's OK. We only want to keep you safe." He was still holding her hand, and leaned over to kiss the top of her head. She started to tremble again as she remembered why she'd fled to Moone in the first place.

"It's really nice of you but I can't..." she began.

"Do you really want to go back to that hotel on your own? What if you black out again? You won't enjoy your vacation if you're constantly worried about passing out when you're on a horse or walking up the mountain or whatever. Why not stay with us for a couple of days until we know you're OK, and then you can go wherever you want?" Travis made it all sound so easy. She swallowed hard.

"Hey, we can even take you out ourselves. There's a band on in town in a couple of days, maybe you'd like to go see it? And we can take you riding whenever you want; Lord knows our horses could do with some exercise! We can even take you to our special spot down near the waterfall. It's real secluded as not many people know it. It's beautiful. I think you'd like it." He smiled at her hopefully and her heart melted.

She sighed. Travis was making a lot of sense.

His hands were as warm as his smile. She smiled back at him and leaned in a little closer. "OK. Just a couple of days, then. But you have to let me earn my keep. I love horses and I'm not a bad cook."

His eyes twinkled as he laughed. "It's a deal." He leaned over to kiss the top of her head just as she looked up at him. They stared into each other's eyes for a minute before his mouth slowly found hers.

Travis licked at the seam until she opened up for him.

She felt his soft, warm tongue steadily explore her mouth and her own tongue reached up to his as they tangled in a sensual dance. She wrapped her hands around his neck and toyed with his tousled, dark curls, which reached his collar. He smelled of musk and of man. Brooke closed her eyes as she lost herself in his embrace. Her pussy tingled and she gasped into his mouth. He pulled her close, and his rock-hard erection dug into her leg.

She felt warm inside, and proud that she had turned him on. That was something she had thought she wasn't capable of. Lost in this sensual world, she felt as though she could do anything. Maybe even...

Suddenly she stiffened and pulled away.

"Hey, what's up?" Travis's deep voice growled to her as he continued to nip at her lip and caress her neck.

"Nothing, it's just that Kent should be back soon. I wouldn't want him to get the wrong impression." Her voice was weak even to her own ears.

Travis chuckled. "And what impression would that be? That we like each other? I think he already knows that. He feels the same way. Is that a problem?"

She frowned. There was no way she could actually *have* both of them. While they were just flirting it didn't matter, but she didn't imagine it could actually lead anywhere. And Brooke was no home wrecker. "But I thought you two were..." She didn't quite know how to say it without sounding offensive.

"We're both bi." Travis smiled as he put her out of her misery.

She sighed, relaxing in his arms.

"And we're not averse to sharing a woman, either. You ever been in a ménage relationship?" Travis tipped her head up so she had to look at him while he asked.

She flushed, shaking her head. "I've heard of them, but I couldn't understand how it wouldn't lead to jealousy or someone feeling left out. Besides, I always wanted a relationship that would last forever." She blushed again, realizing how stupid her last remark must have sounded.

"You don't think a ménage could last forever?"

She was surprised by the serious expression on his face.

"Well, no," she answered truthfully. "I know people have them for one-night stands and stuff, but I've never really been like that." She started pulling away.

"Quite a few of the locals around here are into shared relationships. They seem to work quite well for some people. One family has been together for over forty years. There's three men and one woman. They're still together nine kids and who knows how many grandkids later." Travis sounded so matter-of-fact, Brooke stared at him.

"Is that *normal*?" Her own question shocked her.

Travis laughed. "What's normal? I suppose everything's normal for somebody. We don't all have to be the same, do we?"

Brooke flushed. "I suppose you're right." She looked down at her hands, which she was slowly removing from his grasp.

"So you don't like having two men looking after you,

taking care of your every need, pleasuring you in ways you can't even imagine?"

Brooke felt a trickle between her legs, and stared into her lap. With no underwear on, she was worried it would show through her jeans. She pulled the long shirt down.

Travis bent his head down to hers. "You haven't answered my question, darlin'."

She stared up at him. "Umm, I don't know. I mean, I've never really thought about it, not *really*." She stammered as her brain raced around in circles trying to come up with an answer.

He chuckled. "Well now, I thought it was every woman's fantasy. I figured you girls thought about it all the time."

"Well, as you said, we don't all have to be the same, do we?" She stood up, carefully pulling the shirt down even farther. "I just need to use the bathroom," she said hurriedly as he started to stand up too.

Once behind the closed door, which she noticed didn't have a lock, she sat down and sighed. Her heart was racing, as were her thoughts. If she stayed, she was sure to grow to like him and Kent even more, and that worried her. It would be hard to say good-bye. Even harder if they had one of those ménage things he was talking about. She felt another rush of liquid between her legs at the thought and was glad she was in the right place to deal with it.

Then it dawned on her. Kent was at the hotel

collecting her things. How well had she hidden the letter? Would he...

"Kent's back at last." Travis yelled from the front room. She took a deep breath, straightened herself out, and went to face the music.

Chapter Three

"I was hoping for some good news," Travis muttered to Kent as he took the groceries into the kitchen. "Oh, I've persuaded Brooke to stick around for a while."

"Just for a couple of days. I hope I won't be in your way?" Brooke tried to smile, but had already caught their anxious expressions and knew something was off.

"Of course not. We'll be glad to have you." Travis threw her a salacious wink, and she blushed at the innuendo.

"Terrific, I'll take your things through." Kent smiled and picked up Brooke's bags.

"It's OK. I can do that." She immediately strode over to her belongings, but Kent was too fast.

"Now my momma'd never forgive me if she knew I'd let a lady carry her own bags," he said with a frown.

"Besides, shouldn't you be resting up? Last time I saw you, you were sparked out on that sofa."

Brooke sighed. She had been hoping to check her things to see if anything had been tampered with. She bit her lip and smiled weakly as Kent carried her bags down the hall.

"He's right. You should be resting." Travis gestured to the sofa, and Brooke slowly sat down, trying not to keep checking the door for Kent to come back.

"I packed up everything I could find," Kent called from down the hall. "Don Montgomery said he'll keep anything I've missed when they service your room and we can collect it later. I hope that's all right."

She could hear that he was still in her bedroom, and her heart hammered, wondering what he was doing in there.

"That's great, thank you. How about some coffee?" She got to her feet and headed for the door, but Travis got their first.

"You just hold on a minute, darlin'. If you want coffee, I'll make you one. You're supposed to be resting, remember?"

With an exasperated sigh she went back to the couch. "I just thought Kent might need one. He looked a bit tired."

"Don't you worry about me, I'm fine, baby." Kent appeared in the doorway and her head shot up.

"How 'bout I make us all some coffee?" Travis left the room while Kent came to sit next to her on the sofa.

"Um, so, was everything OK after the storm?" She scanned her eyes over Kent's body.

Kent sat back into the opposite corner of the couch. His pale green eyes narrowed as he studied her studying him. She fidgeted a little, feeling nervous.

"The roads are mainly passable, and there doesn't seem too much damage in town. A couple of trees came down and quite a few tiles have been blown off roofs, but that's about it." Although he answered her question, she got the impression he was just humoring her. She nodded.

"I thought I might go down and see Mr. Hammond later. I just need to check that Blackie's OK after last night. He was real spooked." Brooke frowned as she thought of the poor horse. Fred Hammond would never forgive her if he'd been hurt.

"Blackie's fine. Travis took him back this morning. Don't you remember?" Kent frowned at her thoughtfully.

"Oh, yes, of course. I'd just like to see for myself, that's all. And I want to apologize to Mr. Hammond." She blushed and was grateful that Travis entered the room just then, carrying a tray.

"I made sandwiches too. I hadn't realized how late it's getting. You must be starving." He smiled at Brooke as he placed the tray on the coffee table and began to pour the coffee.

"What time is it?" Brooke wasn't sure how long she'd

been unconscious but guessed it must have been a while if Kent had already been to town and back.

"A little after two." Travis handed her a plate of sandwiches.

"I got talking to Don Montgomery back at the hotel." Kent sipped his coffee.

Brooke stared at the food in her hand as her heart pounded.

"I can't imagine he's too busy down there right now," Travis said.

"No, he's got no one staying there for a few days now that we've hijacked his best customer." Brooke could feel Kent staring at her as he spoke.

"It's only for a couple of days," she reminded him.

"How long were you planning on staying there?" Kent obviously tried to make the question sound innocent, but Brooke felt as though she was being interrogated.

"Just a few days. I hadn't really decided." She shrugged as casually as she could manage. Her heart thudded and she breathed deeply to quell the panic welling up in her. How much did he know?

Kent nodded. "He said you could leave your car there as long as you want. He's keeping an eye on it for you."

The car! She took a long sip of her coffee to buy herself some thinking time. "That's real nice of him. I appreciate that."

"I told Don what happened to you, and that you wouldn't be up to driving for a while, otherwise he was going to bring it up for you." Kent was still studying her. She squirmed under his gaze and the realization she wasn't going to be able to leave town for a while.

"Where did you say you were from again?" Kent clearly wasn't giving up.

She hadn't and he knew it! "Chicago."

"Do you work there?" Travis sat forward, taking a sudden interest. *Damn!*

"Yes. I work in an admin office for a large manufacturing company." She took the last sip of her coffee.

"What do you manufacture?"

She huffed. "All sorts of things. Would it be OK if I went outside for some air now?" She put her dishes on the tray and slowly got to her feet.

"I need to check on the horses. You can come with me if you like." Travis immediately stood up and followed her to the door.

"Here, you'd best put this on." In the hallway he took a large brown coat from the hook and held it up for her. It was a heavyweight Carhartt work coat with a corduroy collar and arctic fleece lining. It swamped her, but it felt soft and warm and smelled of him. She took a deep breath, enjoying his masculine scent. It gave her a small thrill knowing that she was wearing something of his. She looked back to the lounge and saw Kent through the open door. He still sat on the sofa, finishing his coffee. His fair curls framed his face beautifully, and he looked so gorgeous sitting there thinking. She felt a little sorry for him.

He was right to be curious about her. After all, his boyfriend had brought home a total stranger and now they felt obliged to look after her. She couldn't blame him for not being happy with the situation. She turned back to Travis, who had put on a Sherpa lined boar suede jacket with a soft Sherpa fleece collar. It was the classic jean-jacket style with brass snaps up the front. He looked edible as she followed him out the door.

It was cold, but she welcomed the bite of the fresh wind on her face. She closed her eyes for a second to savor it before descending the wooden steps. Travis put a hand out to her, which she took gratefully. The last thing she wanted to do was fall and let them think she was totally incompetent.

It was a sprawling ranch with the main stables over to one side of the house. A smaller stable block stood a little farther away. The wind had blown shrubs and branches around the yard and kicked up the dust.

"Are you OK?" Travis's words cut into her brooding thoughts.

"Yes." Her response was automatic. She had gotten used to always having to be OK.

"Then why are you crying?"

She stopped in the middle of the yard and stared up at him. His big, brown eyes looked worried, and he put an arm around her. She was beginning to realize how much she liked it when he touched her. She took a step back, shrugging his arm off, and wiped her face. To her dismay, she had tears streaming down her cheeks. She hadn't even realized.

"It's just the wind in my eyes." She sniffed, took a deep breath, and strode toward the stables.

A large gray nodded over the door of his stall, and Brooke reached up and gently patted his nose. The horse gave a huff, and she felt his warm breath on her. She leaned in, snuggling into its comfort. Safer to take comfort from a horse than a man.

She could hear Travis's footsteps and his soft, deep voice as he spoke to the horses and checked them over. She heard him rustling about with straw, and the smell of it took her back to her childhood and long summers spent on her grandparents' ranch. A lump formed in her throat, and she coughed to try to remove it. Her thoughts of happier times usually helped to cheer her up, but today she just wanted to cry. Things had changed so much lately.

"Hey, Travis. You checking up on me?"

Brooke heard the stranger's voice and quickly wiped her face in the horse's soft mane before turning around. A guy with a black hat and red checkered shirt stood at the door of one of the stalls a little farther down.

Travis chuckled. "Just making sure everyone's got what they need."

Brooke blushed.

"We're all fine here." The young man was patting the horse next to him. "You going to see the band this week? I heard they're pretty good."

Travis nodded. "Yeah, we thought we'd take our guest with us. Hal, you haven't met Brooke Adams yet, have you? Brooke, this is Hal Jones, he kinda runs this place." Travis gestured toward her and she walked over, trying her best to smile.

"Hello," she said. Hal gave her a dazzling smile in return and shook her hand.

"Well, where've they been hiding you, sunshine?"

"Oh, they were good enough to take me in for a couple of days after I had a riding accident. I'm only here until tomorrow." Brooke felt Travis staring at her but kept her gaze on the young man in front of her.

"Aw, that's a shame. There's a band on in town in a couple of days, The Brandon Boys. We don't get much live music 'round here, 'cept Jonah and his guitar, so it's kind of a big deal. D'you like country music?" Hal chattered on, apparently oblivious to Travis's dark expression.

"Yes, I do." The truth was she *loved* country music and would give anything to see a live band. "But I have to be going tomorrow. Maybe I'll catch up with them another time." She gave Hal a smile. He was really good-looking.

"Looks like the wind's getting up again. Time to batten down the hatches." Travis was already fastening one of the stable doors as he spoke, and Hal jumped into action.

"Yes, sir. I'll get the others to help. Why don't you take Brooke inside? It's getting cold out here." Hal whistled, and Brooke saw a couple of men in the distance, walking toward them.

"OK." Travis held out a hand to Brooke, who reluctantly took it. He sure was showing her who the boss was around here as he marched her toward the house. She had a hard job keeping up with his long strides, but she shuffled along the best she could. He stopped when they reached the porch.

"Just a minute." He leaned her back against the side of the house and put his massive arms on either side of her. His big, dark eyes looked disappointed and hurt, but his chin was stern and angry. "What's all this about you leaving tomorrow?"

Brooke did her best to look innocent. She gave him a puzzled frown. "You said I could stay a couple of days. I arrived yesterday. Besides, I've got places to go. I'm on vacation, remember?"

He narrowed his eyes a little. "Aren't you happy here?"

"Well..." she faltered.

"I'm listening."

"I don't think Kent likes me. He's your boyfriend and you should put him first. I don't want to come between you. I think it's best I go."

To her amazement, Travis chuckled. "Just what makes you think he doesn't like you? He was the one that invited you to stay in the first place, as I recall."

"I know, but I don't think he trusts me. He keeps

asking me questions." It sounded feeble even to her own ears.

Travis chuckled again. "That's just his nature, darlin'. He's interested, that's all. Wants to get to know you better, same as I do. You got a problem with that?" Travis's eyes were twinkling at her now, and his lips had turned up into a sexy smile. She sighed. He really was gorgeous, and she loved being this close to him. His manly scent surrounded her, and she felt oddly safe. Both men seemed to have this effect on her. She didn't think she'd ever feel safe around a man again, let alone two!

She smiled back at him and shook her head.

"Well that's good, 'cause we're planning to take you to see the band in a couple of days, so you've gotta stick around for that, d'ya hear?" His lips were dangerously close to hers, and she felt her breathing get heavier. He slowly closed in on her, and his lips nibbled at her, requesting entry, before plunging in and devouring her mouth. Her pussy clenched as he ran his hands through her hair and he kissed her so forcefully she had to hold on to him for balance. Heat flared through her and she gasped. Slowly she lifted her hands up to his shoulders, and slipped her fingers under his hat to play with his dark waves. Even through their coats she could feel his body press against hers, and the hardness of his erection dug into her thigh. Her pussy was becoming even wetter, but somehow it didn't matter. As his kiss lovingly assailed her mouth, her passion mounted and she lost herself in the moment.

It was only when the wind howled around the corner of the house and whipped the rocking chair onto its side that Travis loosened his grip. Brooke sighed at the loss as he slowly pulled himself away from her.

"You'll be the death of me," he growled as he straightened his jacket. He gave her a wicked wink and she blushed again. "Come on, let's get you warmed up." He opened the door, and she dodged under his muscular arm to go through.

"You just did that," she whispered into his ear as she passed him, and squealed when she felt a swat on her behind.

Travis helped her with her coat and then went to light the fire in the lounge.

"Is it OK if I take a shower?" she asked, desperate to put on some underwear.

"Of course, darlin'. You need any help?"

She flushed and her pussy clenched again. "No, I can manage, thank you."

Brooke was relieved to get out of the baggy clothes and reveled in the hot water that streamed over her body. She picked up a bottle of something and smelled it. It was flowery, fresh and spring-like, not at all overpowering. She rubbed some onto her skin and enjoyed the scent all around her. She wondered why the two guys would have feminine toiletries in their spare bedroom and sighed. Travis had told her they liked to share their women, so perhaps they did it a lot.

As the warmth soothed her aches and bruises, Brooke

found herself relaxing and her mind wandered. Closing her eyes, she tried to imagine what it would be like to have two men at once. Travis had already shown her what an amazing kisser he was, and she liked the thought of that luscious mouth all over her body—her breasts, her nipples, her pussy.

Kent had been very kind to her, but hadn't shown any interest in her physically. Probably the strong, silent type. She imagined Kent standing behind her as Travis kissed his way up and down her front. Kent's massive cock would dig into her butt, and he would caress her back, then her shoulders. He would plant warm kisses on her neck and throat and would nibble at her ears.

As she washed her torso, she ran her hands up and down it, imagining they were the hands of the two guys. As her body flared, she slipped two fingers into her soaking pussy. She slid one over her clit while she pressed the other into her. She imagined it was Travis's tongue, probing her and nipping her clit. With a loud gasp, she came and reached out to the wall for support as the fire ripped through her. She stood panting for a while, letting the soft water wash over her.

Once she'd calmed down enough to step out of the shower, Brooke opened her bag and took out a pair of jeans and a sweater. She smiled when she found her underwear, and quickly got dressed. As she combed her hair, she was surprised to see the face that stared back at her from the mirror. She hadn't noticed before how tensed up she had been, but she could see that now even the muscles in her face seemed to have relaxed a little. Her mind drifted, and she tried to remember when she had last gotten herself off. It had been a long time ago.

He had called himself a Dominant and told her she was his submissive. At first she had been excited to try out a D/s relationship, as she had read about them in books and loved the idea. She had done some research on the internet about the dynamics and how it should work and even spoken to a friend who was happy in the life-style. When she had first been flogged by Chad, she was amazed at how liberating it had felt, and she was surprised that it didn't actually hurt that much. It wasn't long before all that changed, though.

His personality altered and she began to fear him. She had waited on him and done everything he asked of her. She even gave up her job to devote more time to his needs. In return, he had tied her up and whipped her whenever the fancy took him. He had penetrated her, but they never made love anymore. He said she was an embarrassment to him and hated her failing him in front of everyone at the club. She always paid dearly for his disappointment in her. She had learned to fake her orgasms after that, and he had bragged to his friends about how great a lover he was that he had managed to "cure her."

She hugged herself and shook her head to try to dispel the memories. She was out of that awful place. Free. For now.

Brooke could hear the shower from the bathroom

down the hall and made her way toward the kitchen. Perhaps she could start preparing vegetables for dinner.

As she passed a door on her left, she heard a loud grunt, followed by what sounded like a cracking noise. She put her ear to the door and listened. There it was again. Her heart was thudding as she slowly opened the door. Her eyes went wide as saucers and her mouth dropped open when she saw the scene inside. She felt herself glow hot, inside and out, and her skin pricked with fear. Kent stood with his back to her, dressed in black leathers and boots, no shirt. His muscles rippled as he moved. He was wielding a large single tail at a sheet of paper on the opposite wall. With each precisely placed stroke he gave a loud grunt as the air was expelled from his herculean body.

Her feet had turned to lead, and she could hear her heart pounding through her body as panic overtook her. After a few more strokes, she managed to tear her eyes away from Kent and shot back out the door. She ran straight into the ripped chest of Travis, who stood, dripping, in nothing but a towel.

Chapter Four

S he put a hand to her mouth to stop herself from screaming as horror gripped her, and he put his warm, strong arms around her. She couldn't stop shaking as she stood sobbing against his hard body. He didn't speak, just stroked her hair and kissed the top of her head gently.

Brooke didn't notice when the sounds from the room stopped and Kent looked around in dismay to see her standing there, quaking in Travis's arms. He laid down the whip and ran a hand through his blond curls now wet with sweat.

Travis deftly scooped her up in his strong arms and took her into the sitting room while Kent headed toward the shower.

"It's all right, darlin'," Travis whispered softly in her ear, "no one's going to hurt you."

Brooke's tear-filled eyes stared up at him. "I have to

go," she announced and tried to remove herself from his lap.

Travis held her firm. "No, you don't. We just need to talk, that's all." His voice was soft but firm, and he rubbed the tears from her blazing cheeks with his large thumbs.

We need to talk. The words bombarded her head like bullets. She knew what those words usually meant. We need to talk about what we're going to do to rectify your bad behavior. We need to discuss why you continue to defy me in front of my friends. We need to consider how you're going to put things right, now that you've completely humiliated me in front of the whole club. But they never talked. *He* talked. He told her what she was going to do, how she was going to behave and then how she was going to suffer. And boy, did she suffer!

She shook her head. She wasn't going through this again. "No."

Travis stared into her eyes, holding her face firmly in his strong hands, forcing her to look at him. His eyes searched hers. "Why don't you want to talk to me, darlin'? What are you afraid of?"

His gentle voice felt like warm sun on cold skin, but his questions made her shudder. She wouldn't fall for that one again. Chad had asked her so kindly and gently when they first got together. He wanted to know what frightened her so he could protect her from it all. Except that he lied! He just wanted to know the best ways to terrify her.

Brooke swallowed hard, closing her eyes. Travis was gorgeous and when he had held her she had actually felt safe. But she wasn't. She should have known better. Taking a deep breath, she opened her eyes again. He was still staring at her, patiently waiting. She lifted her head slightly and jutted out her chin.

"I can't stay here. I don't feel safe." She spoke calmly and deliberately. No way was he going to be able to accuse her of being too upset to make decisions, or too emotional to think straight. She could see the disappointment in his eyes but wouldn't let herself be swayed. Chad used to use his puppy-dog eyes on her whenever she told him she was unhappy or wanted to leave. She had fallen for it every time. Well, she wasn't going to fall for it again.

Defiantly, she stared back into his eyes. They were so gorgeous—big and dark. She could hardly bear the sadness she saw there. But she had to. Chad had been gorgeous too. Chad had looked sad just before she gave in and then he just looked angry. And he beat her. She couldn't risk going through it again. She deserved better. It had taken her ages to realize it, but she deserved to feel safe. To be happy.

Slowly, Travis slid his hands down her face and away from her body. "I can't argue with that, darlin'," he said quietly. "Kent and I would never harm you, but if you don't trust us enough to believe that, then you just need to do whatever you have to." He backed away from her, giving her some personal space.

Brooke sighed. A massive lump stuck in her throat,

and she wanted to cry all over again. But she couldn't. He was finally letting her go. But it hurt. She felt bereft. Although it was her decision, it wasn't what she wanted. But it was what she needed. She needed to be safe.

She slowly stood and made her way to the door. She was grateful to hear the shower still running as she went to the guestroom and gathered her things. She hadn't even unpacked, so it didn't take long.

As soon as she headed back up the hallway she could hear raised voices from the lounge. *Damn!* Kent had obviously finished up in the shower. She had to pass that room in order to reach the front door, and there was no other way out. Taking a deep breath, she made her way toward the front of the house, hoping their shouting would cover the sound of her leaving.

"How in hell was I supposed to know you'd come back? Last I heard, you'd gone to see to the horses. I thought you'd be out riding for hours. I was hoping to have worked my way out of my funk before you got back. I know I acted like an asshole, but I thought I could make amends with dinner when you two got back here. I never expected you to let her go!" Kent had obviously heard the news. He stood in nothing but a tight pair of blue jeans, his back to the door.

"What else could I do? She's got a right to feel safe, and she sure doesn't feel safe with you around, asking questions and throwing whips all over the place! And did it have to be a *single tail*? I told you about those marks on her..." Travis stopped abruptly as he caught sight of

Brooke standing in the doorway. Her face had turned white as she stared at him. He took a step toward her, as though he were afraid she was going to faint. She took a step back. He stopped.

Kent turned to see what his lover was looking at. He sighed. "Look, baby, why don't you come and..."

Brooke slowly shook her head, still staring at Travis. Her eyes filled with tears and her heart pounded. He'd seen! He'd seen her body! Her grip tightened on her bags, and she marched to the front door. She was out of it and down the steps before either of them spoke.

"Well done keeping *that* secret," Kent said with a superior look.

"Don't you dare blame this on me! If she hadn't seen you with that dang whip, she'd still be here!" Travis seethed and felt his face flush.

"I could have convinced her to stay if you hadn't opened your big mouth about those scars." Kent shook his head. "So, are we going after her or what?"

Travis slumped onto the sofa. "There's no point. We've scared her half to death and betrayed her. Why would she want us now?"

"So you're givin' up, right?"

"Don't you dare!"

"That's what it looks like to me." Kent slowly sat in the chair opposite and closed his eyes.

"You know full well how I feel about her. I really thought we could make it with her, you know? Damn it. I know it's too soon, but I think I'm falling in love with that girl." Travis rubbed his eyes angrily as tears formed.

"And you think I'm not?" Kent opened his eyes and leaned forward.

Travis sniffed. "You hardly touched her. She thinks you don't even like her. And now..."

"I know." Kent sighed ruefully. "It's my fault. I've blown it for all of us. I knew I sounded mean keeping on asking questions, but I really need to know what's going on, you know? I was so annoyed with myself afterward, I figured some exercise might help me see straight."

"And did it?"

"Hell yeah. I'd acted like such an asshole. We know something bad happened to her and she's not going to talk about it until she's ready. She doesn't know yet if she can trust us, let alone confide in us. She just needs some time, that's all. My pushing her for answers was just pushing her away, and that's the last thing I wanted to do. I want her to join our family too. I'm just not as good at showing it as you."

Travis held a hand out to him, and Kent flew into his arms. Travis felt his lover's wet hair brush against him, and he devoured the fair man in a sensual kiss. Kent's tongue teased his own and they both moaned as they held each other closer.

"What are we going to do about her?" Kent asked,

slowly pulling back. "It's getting dark. We can't leave her to walk down the mountain on her own."

"She won't accept a ride from either of us if we offered," Travis groaned as he ran a hand through his dark waves. "Hang on. Why don't I get Hal to pick her up? He's not exactly a stranger and she won't know we sent him."

Kent chuckled, his green eyes twinkling. "Do it."

Travis dashed back to the bedroom and hauled on his Levis, then went outside and saw Hal in the distance. He was in his pickup driving toward the house. Travis waved to him.

"Hey, I was just coming to see you." Hal grinned at his friend. "I need to get this winch repaired. Ned Tucker said he'd take a look at it. I was just on my way down there now, thought I'd drop it off on my way home. That OK with you?"

"Fine. Just do me a favor while you're at it, would you? Brooke's gone. We had words and..."

"She won't want to be out in this weather. Looks like the storm's coming back tonight." Hal shook his head as he looked toward the track. "You want me to bring her back here?"

"I wish! No, she won't want that. I just want to make sure she's safe, that's all. Can you pick her up and take her to the hotel for me? Try to persuade her to stay there tonight. My guess is she'll be planning to get in her car and drive off, but I don't want her out in this." Travis looked to the sky. It was getting dark and the wind was worse than before. The storm was definitely on its way back.

Hal nodded. "Don't worry. I'll find her. I'll give you a call later."

Travis nodded as Hal's pickup joined the track that led down the mountain. Brooke couldn't have gotten far, and it was a straight road, so she should be easy to spot. He went back into the house, where Kent was serving up the casserole he had prepared earlier.

"Hope you're hungry. I was cooking for three." Kent held out a chair for Travis to sit down. Travis rolled his eyes at the chivalry. It was a constant struggle between them, defining who was the more dominant. They badly needed a sub to look after. He smiled and sat down. The smell was divine and suddenly reminded him how hungry he was.

The phone rang as they were clearing away the dishes. Travis leapt over to it, nearly knocking into a chair in his hurry. He sounded cheerful as he answered the caller, so Kent continued washing the dishes. After a few minutes, Travis reached his big arms around his partner's waist, and Kent felt hot breath on the back of his neck.

"I take it that was Hal?" Kent chuckled as he put the last of the plates on the drainer.

"Yup. Brooke's staying at the hotel tonight. And that's not all."

"Well go on. I can see you're dying to tell me!"

"Stella's back. Hal had a word with Don, and he's

gonna get Stella to have a word with her, you know, girl stuff."

"And that's good because?" Kent swiveled around to face his handsome lover, a big smile on his tanned face.

"Hell, you know Stella loves the bones of us. She'll put in a good word with Brooke, won't she? Convince her we're not so bad." Travis beamed.

"You speak for yourself, cowboy. I intend to be *real* bad tonight," Kent replied.

Travis hardened against him and Kent grinned.

Kent wasted no time in urging his lover down the hall. He'd fucked up royally today, and his stomach churned with mixed emotions. One thing was for sure, though; he wasn't going to fuck up tonight. No siree. Tonight he would rein back some control. He would make sure there were no misunderstandings, no suspicions. He knew Travis was every bit as dominant as he was, but tonight Travis would take direction from him. The guys had been together for nearly ten years now and knew darn well when one needed to take charge. And boy, did he need to take charge tonight. They always gave each other what they needed, except the one thing neither could give —a submissive woman. That was the one thing that would make them whole. And Kent was all too aware he had just turned their chances to shit.

"I'm all yours, bud." Travis stood next to their huge bed, wearing nothing but a wicked grin.

Kent's gut clenched. Travis was gorgeous. How had he missed seeing him undress? He badly needed to get a grip. His mouth watered and he swallowed hard. He watched Travis lean over and light a candle on the nightstand. It flickered in the half-light, projecting dancing shadows around the room and over Travis's naked body. His jaw was accentuated as he smiled in Kent's direction, and his muscles rippled as he straightened up and folded his strong arms across that massive, ripped chest. Travis cocked a sexy eyebrow. "Need some help there, buddy?"

Kent suddenly realized that he had just been standing there staring like a prize prick. *Shit!*

With a throaty chuckle, Travis took a step toward him. He stroked Kent's enormous cock through his tented jeans.

Feeling the heat sear through his throbbing member, Kent hissed and grabbed Travis's hands just as they freed him from his discomfort. So much for taking control. "Shower, now!" Kent's command was low and deep.

Travis's eyes appeared almost black as they darted up to meet his. Still grinning, the cowboy backed away from the huge cock that had sprung to attention in his capable hands, and he winked before heading down the hall. Although each of the bedrooms had its own en suite bathroom, the boys preferred the massive one purposely built at one end of the hallway.

Kent took a calming breath after removing his Levis

and followed him out the door. Steam was already rising from the shower when he arrived, and he gaped in awe at the dripping, naked body before him.

Travis turned slightly on hearing him arrive and looked him up and down with approving desire flashing in his eyes.

The smell of Armani and Travis welcomed him into the shower, and he stood behind his partner, drinking him in as lust seared through his veins. Kent leaned into his lover's ripped back, resting his head on the man's shoulder. Travis was a good couple of inches taller than he, and they fit each other perfectly.

Kent's hard cock teased the soft flesh of Travis's gorgeous ass, eliciting a hopeful gasp from the handsome cowboy. He wrapped his strong arms around Travis's body, stroking the soft hairs of his chest and pulling on his nipples before venturing farther south. Kent could feel Travis's heartbeat quicken as he ran his soft hands over his lover's dripping-wet body, and Travis began to pant as Kent's fingers gripped his massive erection.

Kent gasped at the velvety-smooth member in his hand; its size never ceased to amaze him. It felt as if it were all bone, hard as a rock, but covered in the softest pile imaginable. His own cock hardened even more, and he angled it to tempt his lover's huge, muscular inner thighs. When dry, the thick hairs there were rough and provided much-needed friction to his pulsating dick, but now the water softened them to a cushion for his cock to rest against.

Kent stood for a minute, letting the boiling-hot water wash over them both. He was left with a feeling of failure and emptiness. The warmth of the huge body in his arms soothed his negativity, and, as his cock twitched, he gradually rose above his emotions and replaced them with determination and power. He had fucked up. Now it was time for him to make amends. And he would.

Travis seemed to notice Kent's breathing become more rapid, and his body tensed in front of him. Kent's cock jerked up and prodded his butt hard, causing Travis to gasp.

Kent bit hard on the back of Travis's neck and yanked on the cowboy's straining cock. With hard strokes, he squeezed his fingers around its thick girth and grinned in contentment as pre-cum drooled down his hand. He heard Travis hiss and knew he felt every sensation. Travis braced himself, placing his hands flat against the wall in front of him.

"Yeah, you better hold on tight, bro," Kent growled into his ear. His voice was feral. It sounded angry and brutal, but Travis would know the true emotion behind it.

"I'm ready for you, buddy."

Kent didn't need telling twice. With one almighty shove, he thrust his hot dick like a poker straight into Travis's tight asshole. They both hissed at the pain. They needed this pain. They needed it as much as they needed air. Kent only stopped when his heaving balls slapped against Travis's ass.

Once Travis's head came up again, as he took a deep breath, Kent knew he was ready to continue. He treated Travis's asshole to a violent barrage of quick, deep strokes while he continued to pump the cowboy's weeping cock.

The steamy air was filled with the sound of groans and murmurs as the two men gave each other everything they needed. Kent's mind turned to grit as he pounded his lover for all he was worth. Travis moaned at the glorious assault on his body. He bore down and pushed back, exulting in the sensations as Kent nailed him tirelessly with his massive cock. He was deliciously stretched in both directions, and luxuriated in the bite of pain that shot through him. Kent pushed all his urgency and passion into his lover, and Travis reveled in it.

Kent dug his fingers into Travis's hip and he gripped him like a vise. He placed the cowboy exactly where he wanted him, and he gave him everything he had. His love was rabid. He bit into Travis's hard flesh, wishing he could get into every part of his lover's taut body. He heard a moan, and Travis's head fell back, rubbing his long wet hair against Kent's flushed face. Kent buried himself in the smell and feel of the man's waves, murmuring into his ear.

"God, I love you, bro. I love you to death, you know that?"

"I know it, bud. I love you too."

Travis's husky moan reverberated from his throat through to Kent's lips. The sensation took Kent over the edge. With one last impalement, he shot his boiling seed right up his lover's ass, letting out a guttural groan. After the first initial burst, he continued to ram Travis's hole until he had given him every drop he had. At the same time, Kent yanked hard on Travis's pulsating cock, causing him to climax in long, thick spurts, which splattered the wall tiles and dribbled down.

Kent slowly rubbed his hand all over Travis's cock, which was hardly what he might call flaccid even after all the exertion! The hand that had clenched his lover's hip loosened and stroked the cowboy's eight-pack, then his hairy chest. Travis moaned, and the tension slowly left his body as he leaned into the ministrations of this sated lover. Kent planted hot kisses all around Travis's neck and around to his collarbone.

The water continued to pour over the guys, soothing their minds as well as their bodies. After a while, they washed each other tenderly, enjoying the feel of skin on skin. Travis faced his partner with sultry desire in his eyes. Kent took in a gulp of breath at the beauty of his lover. He slowly reached up to meet his mouth and he gently nibbled at the cowboy's full bottom lip. Travis opened his mouth to welcome him in, and their tongues tangled and swirled as their hands roamed each other's hot, wet spent bodies. Before long they were making their way back down the hall. Neither had said a word since coming, but Kent knew Travis felt his loving presence in his headspace just as strongly as he felt Travis's in his.

The candle was almost melted when they climbed

into their huge bed. Kent sighed as they lay in each other's arms.

Travis pulled his head back slightly to look at him. His dark eyes searched his lover's gorgeous face. "You OK, bud?" Travis's voice was low and sensual.

"I am now, bro." Kent gave his partner a dazzling smile. "And I'll be even better when we've got our girl back." He snuggled into Travis's tanned, hard chest, still smiling as he closed his eyes. He could almost feel Travis's devious mind plotting ways to make their dream come true.

Chapter Five

Tears flooded Brooke's eyes as she ran across the yard and onto the track. It was getting dark, but she didn't care. She just had to get out of there. She couldn't believe that she had already started to have feelings for those men. She didn't even know them. They had seemed so kind and tender. Travis had touched her and made her feel safe; Kent was more reserved, but really seemed to care about her. She shook her head to try to rid it of her thoughts.

The track was uneven and she stumbled a few times, blinded by her tears and distracted by her speculations. She sniffed as she managed to save herself from falling one more time, and angrily wiped her eyes.

She took a few deep breaths and tried to think rationally. If she could get to the hotel in town, she could pick up her car and be out of this place tonight. She gazed at the scenery around her. The trees looked black against the inky-blue sky, and the mountains appeared more rounded than jagged. She could hear the shushing of the waterfall nearby, and a few birds chirping their good-nights to each other. She loved the tranquility of this place and would be sad to leave it.

She had only been here for a few days but had already fallen in love with the area. The people seemed so friendly and welcoming, and she had actually felt as though she could belong here. The sound of a car behind her made her jump, and she instinctively moved into the verge. Her heart beat faster when it stopped just in front of her. It wasn't green, like Travis's pickup, and for a second she wasn't sure if that didn't disappoint her a little.

"Hey, Brooke."

She sighed with relief that the person inside obviously knew her, and she found his voice a little familiar. As she caught up with the vehicle, she recognized Hal's hat as he hung out the window, waving to her. He had the most incorrigible grin, and she couldn't help smiling back at him.

"Hal, what're you doing here?" She was surprised at how relieved she was to see him.

"Gotta take this here winch to Ned Tucker's place. I reckon the motor's dead, so he's going to check it out for us. You need a ride to town?" Hal Jones was so laid-back and friendly, Brooke couldn't help liking him.

She hadn't realized what a long trek it would be to reach town from all the way up here. She had ridden up on horseback and it didn't seem half as far. She nodded, grateful for the lift. "That would be great if it's no trouble...?"

"I'd be glad for the company." He smiled at her as he took her bags and stowed them under the bench seat at the front of the pickup.

Brooke ran around and jumped in the other side. It was warm in the cab, and she liked the smell of oil that permeated the air.

"Thought I'd drop in on Uncle Don on my way. You going to the hotel?" Hal drove steadily down the rough track.

"Uncle Don? You're related to Mr. Montgomery?" Brooke stared at him in surprise. He chuckled.

"Yep. Uncle Don's my momma's brother. Why? Can't see any resemblance?" He grinned at her.

"To be honest, no. I suppose maybe your hair, but he's so..."

Hal chuckled again. "Bossy?"

Brooke blushed. She hadn't wanted to say the word, but he'd hit the nail squarely on the head. She nodded.

"Oh, he comes across as the big bad Dom, but he's a p—kitten really." Hal nearly stumbled over his words.

"Big bad Dom?" Brooke frowned.

"Yep, Don the Dom they call him. He's a real hardass Dominant but you wouldn't know it if you saw him today. Aunt Stella's coming home tonight, and he's running around like a headless chicken. Wants to make sure the place is perfect for her. He's had the staff running all over the place making sure everything's just right."

"Why? Is she bossy too?" Brooke hadn't yet met Mrs. Montgomery but understood that she had been visiting her sick mother for a week or so.

Hal chortled. "Hell, no. She's the sweetest woman you could meet. That's why Uncle Don loves her so much. He just wants everything to be right for her, you know?"

"Oh." Brooke frowned.

"What's up?" Hal noticed her expression.

"Well, if she's his submissive, shouldn't *she* be the one worrying about having everything right for *him*? It seems the wrong way around to me." Brooke was surprised that she had the nerve to ask the question really, but it just kind of came out. Hal was so easy to talk to.

Hal laughed again. "You don't know much about D/s relationships, I take it?"

Brooke flushed. "Yes I do, actually," she informed him indignantly.

Hal stopped laughing and cleared his throat. "Well in that case, you'll know that it's full of give and take. Each partner giving each other what they need. Aunt Stella would hate to come home to a mess, and Uncle Don doesn't want to give her the impression the place falls apart the minute her back's turned. They love each other; they want to make each other happy."

"But if he's her Dominant, isn't it *her* job to keep *him* happy?" Brooke frowned again.

"Of course. And as her Dominant, it's *his* place to make *her* happy." Hal spoke slowly. Brooke said nothing.

"That storm's brewing up again. Are you staying at the hotel tonight?" He glanced up at the dark sky as a few large drops of rain splattered onto his windshield.

"No, I'm going tonight. I have to pick up my car from the hotel, though, if you're headed that way?"

"Going where? It's not going to be safe driving tonight, sunshine."

Brooke felt herself flush. She didn't actually know where she was headed next, but just felt that she should leave town. Things were too complicated here.

Hal sighed. "The storm's settling in for the night, maybe even a couple of days. You'd be safer staying at the hotel until it's passed. In a couple of hours the roads in and out of town will be cut off. It often gets like that up here. At least if you're in town you'll have everything you need right there."

Brooke bit her lip. She hadn't contemplated staying another night at the hotel, but she could see the sense in what he said. Besides, if the town was cut off by the weather, at least it would mean that Chad wouldn't be able to catch up with her for a while. She would be safe.

Hal drew up outside the hotel. It was only a small building with a few rooms, but it was homey and she liked it there.

"Looks like Aunt Stella made it home," he said, looking at a small yellow car in the parking lot. "Uncle Don'll be relieved about that."

Brooke got out of the truck. "Thank you so much for the ride." She smiled up at Hal as he carried her bags inside.

"No problem. It wasn't exactly out of my way." He winked at her, making her blush. "Hey, Uncle Don, I've brought your customer back for you." He chuckled as Don Montgomery appeared from the dining room.

"Nice to see you again, Miss Adams. Do we have the pleasure of your company again tonight?" Don was a big man with a powerful voice, which frightened Brooke a little, but he had a nice smile and had always been kind to her.

"Yes, sir, if that's all right?" He must have thought her a total fool, having her things taken up to the ranch only this morning and now appearing back here again already. She was dreading the inevitable questions that were bound to be asked.

Don Montgomery seemed totally unperturbed. "Of course. Same room as before? Or you can move if you prefer? All the rooms have been serviced." The hotelier was obviously proud of his efforts, which made Brooke smile.

"The same room would be fine, thank you." She took the key and Hal handed over her bags.

"Why don't you go and get settled and then have dinner with my wife and me? We've got no other guests staying tonight."

"I've already eaten actually, sir. Thank you for the offer anyway. I might have a sandwich later on if that's all right, though?" No doubt he'd been looking forward to his wife's return and had probably planned a private dinner for the two of them tonight.

"Well, if you're sure? Maybe come down for a drink with us in an hour or so? My wife would love to meet you."

"I will. I look forward to meeting her too," she assured him as she turned to go. "Thanks again, Hal," she called over as she reached the stairs.

The guy tipped his hat in acknowledgement and leaned over to speak to his uncle.

Brooke made her way upstairs and walked into the room she had left yesterday morning. She loved this little room. It had a wonderful view of the mountain up ahead, with lots of pine trees at its foot. She could see a few houses, but the majority of the town was at the other side of the hotel. She enjoyed the seclusion.

She put her bags on the floor and threw herself onto the soft bed. The room only had a few pieces of furniture, but it was plenty. She promised herself she would put her clothes back in the drawers later. There wasn't anything that needed to be hung in the wardrobe. All she had taken was a few pairs of jeans and shorts and a stack of T-shirts. She only had a couple of sweaters with her, and her coat had been left in the car.

She sighed as she thought of the little home she had left behind. It was only a small apartment but she had loved it there, at first. She hadn't made much money at her admin job, but she had enough to get by and make her home nice and cozy.

After Chad had moved in, he had insisted on heavy net curtains at every window to afford them some privacy. He said she must have been an exhibitionist for not having them before, despite being on the eighth floor. He had criticized her for not having enough money to furnish the place with everything new. Soon after that, he insisted that she give up her job as he said it was keeping her away from him too much. She had to let go of all her friends too, as he felt they were a bad influence on her. She had ended up completely cut off from the outside world. Then things got really bad.

He told her it was his place now as he was paying for everything, and he had his friends around for drinks and parties whenever he wanted. She was always afraid of his friends; they seemed very aggressive, especially when they had all been drinking. Kenny would always pick an argument with someone or other and fists would fly. Jacko and Trent were another couple of evil bastards who would use any excuse to get in a fight. Chad was aggressive too. He used to beat her for no good reason, often in front of his friends, who sat around laughing while she wept and cried out for help. When they went to the local BDSM club, Chad took great delight in keeping her on a leash and never missed an opportunity to punish her.

Then, one night it was too much. Chad had been drinking again and had taken things too far. She had woken in the hospital; someone had found her and called emergency services. The police had asked all sorts of questions, and she told them everything. She had to, she had no choice. They couldn't find Chad. He seemed to have disappeared into thin air.

When she recovered, she crept back to the apartment. He had been back and trashed the place. She quickly took some clothes and stuffed them into a couple of bags before heading for the door. Then she saw him. Not Chad. This was one of his drinking buddies, Kenny. She'd seen him here loads of times, leering at her. He had that horrendous look on his face now as he blocked her doorway. He also had a knife.

"Chad wants you to sign this." He handed her a piece of paper. It was neatly typed and clearly explained that she had lied about all her accusations. It stated that she had only incriminated Chad to get him into trouble because he had threatened to finish with her. She tasted bile in her mouth as she read the words through tear-filled eyes. The police had promised her she would be safe. They would catch him and lock him up. She could start her life again. They lied. She wasn't safe now. The ugly fucker waved his knife at her while he watched her expectantly. "I ain't got all day, whore!"

She screamed. She opened her mouth wide and yelled for all she was worth. She could hear someone coming up the steps to the apartment, and her heart leapt. Unfortunately the fucker turned on his heel and ran.

Brooke stuffed the letter in her bag and ran down the steps. She climbed into her car and pulled away. She was just in time to see Chad skulking down the street, half-hidden by a garage, obviously waiting for his friend to return with the letter all signed.

She recalled her heart pounding as she slammed her foot on the accelerator and hightailed it out of town. Even if she showed the police the letter, they couldn't do anything. They couldn't find him, couldn't stop him. But *he* could find *her*.

As Brooke lay staring at the ceiling, she was suddenly aware of the tears that had begun to stream down her cheeks. The cozy room suddenly felt too big and open, too exposed. For a few hours today she had felt safe.

The image of Kent wielding that whip gripped her. She hadn't seen his face but had imagined he had been angry. His muscles had rippled as he raised his arm. That immense power was arousing, but she could never trust a man to wield it for her again.

Her head was pounding and she closed her eyes. Curling herself into a ball, she snuggled into a pillow and sobbed before falling fast asleep.

When she awoke it was pitch-black in the room, and she had to think for a moment to decipher where she was. She leaned over and switched on the bedside lamp. It was nearly ten. Her mind raced as she remembered her promise to meet up with Mr. and Mrs. Montgomery, and she jumped off the bed and went to refresh herself. She grabbed her wash things from the bag on the floor and tidied herself up before rushing downstairs.

"There you are." Don Montgomery looked very

smart in a black suit and tie. Brooke felt a little scruffy in her jeans and sweater, but there was nothing she could do about it now. She was glad she had at least had a wash and tied her hair up. He stood at the little bar, serving a couple of glasses of something sparkling, and automatically grabbed another glass.

Mrs. Montgomery sat at one of the small tables in the corner of the bar. She was a large lady and wore a bright red dress. Her hair was dark and fastened to the top of her head with a big, sparkly clip. She had a broad smile, and her eyes lit up when she spotted Brooke.

Brooke walked nervously across the bar and smiled at them both. Mr. Montgomery placed the three glasses on a silver tray, and Brooke followed him over to the table.

"Stella, this is Brooke Adams. She's been staying with us for a few days. Brooke, this is my wife, Stella." Don Montgomery sounded very official as he made the introductions.

"How lovely to meet you, dear. Come and sit by me." The lady held out her hand and gave Brooke's a warm shake before urging her over to sit next to her.

"It's lovely to meet you too, Mrs. Montgomery."

"Call me Stella. I hear you're practically one of the family. Don tells me you had an accident yesterday. Are you all right?" Stella wore bright red lipstick to match her dress, and her mouth smiled widely as she spoke. Brooke felt her warmth.

"Yes, I'm fine, thank you. I fell off a horse and got a few bumps and bruises, that's all." Brooke nodded to Mr.

Montgomery as she took a glass of wine from the tray and tasted it. Champagne. They must be celebrating tonight.

"And you were found by the boys up on the ranch. Doc Hardy has been to see you and told you to rest for a few days. Are you going to do that here?" Stella had been well informed.

"I had a restful day today." Brooke hoped that would suffice. It didn't.

"And tomorrow?" Don Montgomery's voice was low and deep, very much like the boys' on the ranch, Brooke realized. She knew he wouldn't be happy if she told him she was hoping to drive off tomorrow, so she decided to play it safe.

"I'll see what tomorrow brings." She smiled sweetly at him and he frowned. Stella giggled.

"Don, dear, how about a few nibbles to go with this?" Stella gave her husband a dazzling smile as she sipped her champagne.

Brooke gaped at Stella's audacity.

"Of course, pet." He gave his wife a small kiss on the top of her head and smiled as he got up and went toward the kitchen.

Without looking at her, Stella put her hand over Brooke's. She hadn't realized she was trembling. She looked away from the kitchen door as soon as the man was gone, and stared back at his wife.

"It's all right, dear, don't worry." Stella's voice was gentle, and Brooke's tremors turned into aftershocks.

"But won't he…"

"He loves me and I love him." Stella smiled at her. "We give each other what we need and what we want. He can't do enough for me, and I feel the same way about him. You've been in a bad relationship, haven't you, dear?"

Brooke gasped and stared at the older lady.

Stella continued to smile. "It's not all one-sided, you know. If a relationship is going to work, you both have to give and take. My guess is you're the one who did all the giving?"

Tears streamed down Brooke's face as she nodded. Stella offered her a handkerchief and put a soothing arm around her. The older lady was all soft and round and gave great hugs.

"What happened at the ranch?"

"Kent had a whip," she whispered.

Stella nodded knowingly. "He's brilliant with a single tail. The best around here. Girls are lining up to have him use it on them at the club. Did he use it on you?"

Brooke shook her head.

"He didn't hurt you, then?" Stella looked a little confused.

"No. No one hurt me. I just got a little scared, that's all." Now that she said it aloud, Brooke realized it really wasn't such a big deal. She took another sip of her champagne. It fizzed in her mouth and she enjoyed the taste. She sniffed, suddenly feeling a little better.

"We all get scared once in a while. Sometimes it's a

good thing." Stella smirked as though a memory had just flashed through her mind. "Those boys wouldn't ever hurt anyone, though. They're great guys."

As Brooke watched Stella take another gulp of her wine, she realized this lady spoke a lot of sense. She obviously knew a lot about the D/s lifestyle too. Brooke wondered what else she knew about.

"They're both gay, aren't they? So which one's the... you know...?" Brooke stammered.

"Travis and Kent are actually bisexual. They're both Dominants too, which makes life a little hard for them. They'll be fine once they find the right girl. They need a nice sub to look after." Stella smiled at Brooke.

"Look after?" Brooke frowned. That didn't make any sense.

"Of course. That's part of a Dominant's job, isn't it? To look after his sub. What did you think their job was?" Stella asked kindly.

"Well, discipline. They tell you what to do and you do it. If you get it wrong, you get punished," Brooke whispered, almost afraid of being overheard, though there was no one else there.

"Sweetie, I hate to tell you this, but you've got it all wrong. Whoever told you that was a relationship was talking out of his ass! It sounds to me like you've been bullied half to death. Did he beat you too?" Stella's voice was soft but firm.

Tears flooded down Brooke's face again and she nodded. Stella pulled her into another big hug, where she sobbed for quite a while before sitting upright. She wiped her face and sniffed hard.

"That's why you were afraid of Kent's whip. What was he doing with it?" Stella asked softly.

"He-he didn't know I was there. He was swiping at some paper on the wall of his...his..."

"Playroom? Dungeon? That room where the boys keep all the kinky stuff. He was probably practicing. Kent's a perfectionist, that's what makes him so good. He won't try anything unless he knows he can do it properly. That way he can't harm anyone." Stella spoke so matter-of-factly it made Brooke stare at her in wonder.

"He was concentrating, I think." Now that Brooke thought it through, she remembered that he was actually studying his stroke and hitting his target very precisely.

Stella nodded and gave her another big hug. "BDSM's not for everyone, and most of us around here don't go to extremes with it, but if you like it there's nothing wrong with it."

"I used to like playing at a club," Brooke blurted out.

"Have you been to Ty's here in town?" Stella asked as they both resumed their drinks.

Brooke stared at her. "You've got a BDSM club here in Moone?"

"We sure have. I'd be happy to take you along there one night and show you what it's really all about if you'd like to? You don't have to do anything; we can just go to watch."

Brooke gasped. "I'd love to. Yes please, I'd love to go

with you." She beamed at the older lady and squeezed her tight.

Stella laughed. She had a wonderful, loud laugh that was infectious. Brooke wiped her face again and giggled, just as Don arrived with a platter full of tidbits. The young girl's stomach rumbled on cue, and she remembered she hadn't eaten yet.

Stella giggled back. "I can see you and me are gonna get along just fine, Brooke. You might even enjoy your stay here at Moone after all," she said with a wink.

Chapter Six

Brooke slept late the next morning. She stared at her watch, horrified. Must have been the champagne. She dived into the power shower, then pulled on her blue jeans and a sweater. She didn't bother with makeup and scraped her thick wet hair up into a bushy ponytail before rushing downstairs.

"Good morning, sweetie." Stella was in the foyer. "Did you have a good sleep?" Her hair was casually piled on top of her head, and she had no makeup on today. She looked like a different person, although her wide smile was still the same.

"Yes, I'm so sorry." Brooke blushed as she spoke.

"What on earth for?" Stella frowned incredulously, "You're supposed to be resting, remember? Doctor's orders, I understand."

"W-well yes, but..." Brooke stammered, unsure of what she really wanted to say.

"Then you're doing the right thing. Come and have breakfast with me." Stella whisked her into the dining room. A waiter was the only person in there. He was polishing cutlery and setting up the tables. He smiled as the ladies swooped in.

"Would you like a cooked breakfast, Brooke?" Stella asked as they took a table by the window.

"No, thank you. Just coffee and toast, please."

Stella frowned. "Well all right, but make sure you eat some lunch today."

Brooke imagined this is what it must feel like to have a mother. Hers had died when she was very young, as had her Dad, and she didn't remember either of them.

The waiter swaggered over to take their order; he looked as though he would be more at home in a saddle than walking.

"Morning, Zak. Could we just have coffee and toast for now, please?" Stella gave him a winning smile, and he grinned at them both before sauntering over to the kitchen.

Brooke frowned when she looked out the window. It was raining hard and the wind was up.

"The storm's set in for a couple of days," Stella said with a sigh. "What are your plans?"

"I don't really know." Brooke bit her lip. She really didn't have clue what to do now. She knew she wouldn't get far if she tried to drive out of town as the roads were probably flooded by now.

"Well now, how much have you seen of our little town?" Stella asked cheerfully.

"Not much," Brooke admitted. "I've been riding a couple of times up the mountain on Mr. Hammond's horse. It's really beautiful up there. I went to the corner shop for some gum a few days ago, but I haven't really looked around yet."

"Well, if you like I can show you around? It's not safe enough to drive or ride horseback, but we can take a stroll together if we wrap up warm." Stella smiled as the waiter laid their breakfast on the table and they both tucked in.

They enjoyed their meal before going upstairs to get ready to face the weather. Stella took an umbrella, and Brooke took her coat from her car on her way out. The town was surprisingly busy, given the conditions.

"Folks must be getting stocked up with supplies in case this weather lasts," Stella explained. "Sometimes we get cut off for weeks when it's real bad."

Brooke looked horrified. "You mean I might not be able to get home?" Her voice trembled.

Stella smiled at her and linked her arm comfortingly. "I don't think it'll be that bad this time. I've seen it far worse than this," she soothed her. "Is someone waiting for you at home, Brooke?"

Brooke felt a lump in her throat. She couldn't tell Stella that she couldn't actually go back home even if the weather improved. "No, I live alone. But I have to get back to work."

"Where do you work?"

"It's a big manufacturing company in Chicago. I work in the admin department."

"How interesting. What do you manufacture?"

"Oh, we make all sorts of stuff there. Primarily rubber products." Brooke waved her free arm dismissively, hoping Stella would change the subject.

"Oh, like tires and things?"

Tires were actually their main export, so Brooke was a little taken aback by the question. "Yes," she replied simply.

"How long have you worked there, sweetie?" Stella looked so innocent as she asked. Brooke took a deep breath to quell her fears and tried to reassure herself that the lady was just being polite and interested.

"A few years," Brooke said with a shrug. "Oh look, is that a clothes shop?"

She had noticed a pretty shop window full of beautiful lingerie.

"Yes, do you want to take a look?"

Stella led her across the narrow road through the center of town. They had to pick their way around the puddles. Shops and offices lined both sides of the street, and people seemed to be hurrying about everywhere. Dirty pickup trucks chugged up and down the road, dropping mud off their heavy treads.

"Good morning." A glamorous lady with long blonde hair stood behind the counter by the door. She was heavily made-up and looked stunning. Her big red lips showed a dazzling smile and perfect teeth.

"Good morning, Melinda. This is Brooke. She's staying at the hotel for a while." Stella smiled as they walked in.

Brooke smiled nervously. Melinda gave her a broad smile in return.

"Well it's nice to meet you, Brooke." Melinda shook her hand. Brooke just smiled back.

"We're just gonna take a look around if that's OK?" Stella ushered Brooke toward a rail of lacy panties.

Melinda nodded and smiled again. She was so pretty and skinny Brooke didn't know what to say to her. She wore a red pencil skirt and a black silk blouse. Brooke couldn't see her feet but guessed she was in high heels. Brooke sighed, feeling very fat and ugly with no makeup and her hair pulled off her face.

I must look like a drowned rat to that gorgeous woman, Brooke thought miserably.

"Satin or lace?" Stella's question pulled Brooke from her thoughts, and she noticed the lovely items in front of her.

"Either." Brooke shrugged, having never considered her preference. Chad had always forbidden her to wear underwear when they were together, so she considered any at all to be a luxury.

As they moved away from the counter, and Melinda's prying ears, Stella murmured to Brooke, "This is where most of us get our outfits for Ty's. There's a lot more stuff toward the back of the shop if you're interested?"

Brooke's eyes lit up and she nodded.

There were some beautiful corsets in satin and lace and exquisite underwear that hardly covered anything.

"Do you have much of this type of stuff?" Stella asked, putting a gorgeous red corset against herself and admiring it in the mirror.

"No...well, not with me," Brooke stammered. It suddenly occurred to her that she had left all of her fet wear behind. In her hurry to escape, she had just grabbed the first clothes at hand, which were mostly what she wore every day. She even had to hunt for some underwear.

She thought back to her "play" wardrobe and frowned. Chad had bought all her clothes for the club and had put her in what he wanted to see, not what she wanted to wear. He bought her really tight, short dresses that pushed her ample bosom up and showed her ass as she walked. Brooke felt horribly self-conscious and was convinced the other women sniggered when they saw her. Chad didn't seem to notice—either that or he regarded it as part of her punishment. The corsets he chose were lacy and itchy, especially when she got hot. He always insisted on tying them too tight so she could hardly breathe, and she had fainted in the club on several occasions, much to his anger.

"Brooke, are you OK?"

She blinked and realized Stella was holding on to

both her arms, staring at her face. She sniffed and was horrified to feel tears pricking her eyes.

"I'm fine." She tried to smile at the older lady and blinked hard to keep back the torrent of unshed tears that threatened to overspill.

"Here." Stella handed her a lace handkerchief. "We can go somewhere else if you'd rather, sweetie?"

"No, no, I'd like to take a look." Brooke was intrigued to see what they had, moreover to see if there was anything that might look half-decent on her curvy frame.

Stella smiled. "Well, if you're sure. They've got some dresses and skirts at the back. Shall we take a look at those?"

Brooke nodded and followed Stella to the very back of the store. Several mannequins were lined up along the back wall, sporting a range of different outfits. Brooke was instantly drawn to a black leather dress with capped sleeves and laces up the front. It was short but didn't appear to be quite as short as the ones she was used to. Not only did she wish to protect her modesty, she was also aware she now had scars at the tops of her legs that she would prefer to hide. What really added to the appeal of the dress was the size of the mannequin wearing it; in fact, she noticed, quite a few of them seemed to cater to the slightly larger sizes.

"Try it on," Stella urged.

Brooke bit her lip but took one from the rail nearby. Stella ushered her into the little changing cubicle in the corner of the shop, and she took a calming breath before putting on the dress. She was stunned to find it fit perfectly. She was so used to finding that although a dress was supposed to be in her size, it was actually far too small.

This one slid on beautifully, and she tied the lace excitedly, then stood back to admire her reflection. She gave a little gasp. It actually looked great! The shape of the bust pushed her bosom up slightly, giving it a lovely round contour, but didn't make it look as though it was falling out. The dress had been cut so that it glided over her tummy and large hips, making her look shapely rather than fat. The length allowed her to move around without showing off tomorrow's washing with every action—a primary concern in an environment where she might not even be allowed to wear that much underwear.

"Is it OK, sweetie?"

Stella gave a massive smile, which told Brooke all she needed to know. Brooke flushed and dived behind the curtain to change back into her jeans.

"That's a definite," Stella said as she took the dress from Brooke, who suddenly realized she hadn't even checked the label. It was bound to cost a fortune.

"I forgot to check the tag," she whispered to Stella as they made their way toward the counter.

"It's my treat." Stella winked at her and handed the dress and the red corset to Melinda.

Brooke blushed, but didn't want to argue in front of the shop assistant.

"Is it still raining?" Stella asked.

Brooke walked over to the door and looked out. "It seems to have stopped." She looked around to see that Stella had already paid and was following her over. Brooke automatically put out a hand and took the shopping bag from her.

"Good. Let's grab some lunch across the road, and then I'll show you where Ty's is. It'll be a quiet night tonight, but I'm sure you'll enjoy it," Stella said with a grin as they left the store.

The guys had woken early on the ranch. After a shower and breakfast, Kent had helped Travis tend to the horses for a while before getting ready to leave for town.

"I won't be long. Just need to pick up a few supplies and thought I'd drop by the office." Kent took Travis's mouth in a lingering kiss before climbing into the pickup. Travis grinned and watched him drive off. He was probably on to him about his plans.

Kent arrived at the hotel and was pleased to hear that Brooke was booked in for another night. "Probably longer if I know Stella," Don Montgomery told him with a wink. "They're off out shopping right now. Stella's keeping a close eye on her, making sure she doesn't overdo it. She's taking her to Ty's tonight if she's up to it. They talked about it last night, and little Brooke was real interested. Said she used to go to a club in Chicago."

"I don't suppose she told Stella which one?"

Don shook his head. "She would've told me. You were right about her being in a tough relationship, though. She was crying quite a bit with Stella last night. I stayed in the kitchen until it was safe to come out."

Kent gave a weak grin. He was sad that Brooke had been upset and he hadn't been there for her, but could well imagine Don the Dom's face when he saw her crying. Don was almost afraid of that much emotion.

"Do you think she'll be well enough to go to the club tonight? She's supposed to be resting," Kent asked with a frown.

"Stella won't take her if she's not up to it, son. Besides, she assured me she just wants to show her around, let her see what it's *really* all about. Your little girl seems to have a very warped view on the subject. Probably understandable. Anyhow, Stella promised me she won't let anything happen to her. Besides, *I'll* be there." Don's voice became a gruff growl as he finished his sentence.

"We'll see you there, then. Much obliged for your help." Kent doffed his hat and heard Don laugh raucously as he left the hotel. Looked like Travis wasn't the only one on to him.

Kent noted Brooke's car in the parking lot outside and took down the license plate. The car was very old and had lots of dents and scratches, some of them quite severe. The oxidation of the scratches indicated that they had been there for some time, and the shape showed that someone had been in quite a hurry when they had gotten them.

He pouted as he made his way down the busy street. Everyone smiled and nodded as he passed them. He suddenly dodged into a shop doorway and grinned. Stella and Brooke were just coming out of the lingerie shop, chatting excitedly.

Brooke was carrying a large bag with the shop's brand emblazoned in glitter along the front. Kent couldn't help wondering what they had been buying, and his heart fluttered a little at the thought of finding out tonight. He watched them cross the street and nodded with approval when he saw they were going to the small diner. Stella was looking after Brooke well. He felt a jolt in his gut and wished he had looked after her better himself. Once they were out of sight, he took the turn that led him to the sheriff's office.

"Well now, you missing us already, deputy?" Sheriff Mason Bains looked up from his desk as Kent strolled in.

"Yeah, right." Kent grinned at his boss. "You on your own?"

"Uh-huh, Jolene's just taking her lunch break. Something wrong?" Mason frowned. He could always see right through Kent's poker face.

"Can you run a check on a car for me?" Kent gave Mason a sheet of paper with the license number written on it.

Mason looked at it and frowned. "Is this something to do with that girl you and Travis found?"

Kent nodded. "Said her name's Brooke Adams. I had a quick look on the internet but I can't find anything. She's from Chicago; works as an admin in a large manufacturing company, but I don't know anything else, except that something's not right."

"You think she's a crook?" Mason frowned.

Kent shook his head. "I doubt it. But she might be in trouble. She's got scars and welts on her body. Travis saw them, thinks some of them might be quite recent."

"You seen them?"

"Nope."

The sheriff nodded slowly and looked back to the piece of paper. "I'll check this out and let you know. She still in town?"

"Yep. Staying at the Montgomery Hotel. I'm hoping this weather'll keep her here long enough for us to find out what's going on."

"I'll get on it right away," Mason promised.

"Much obliged to you, boss." Kent nodded and left the office. He hurried back up the street, careful to reach his pickup at the hotel without Brooke seeing him. He couldn't wait to tell Travis that they had a chance for a date with her tonight.

Chapter Seven

Ty's was nothing like the clubs Brooke had visited in Chicago. Although it was obviously a BDSM club with dark walls, loud music, and the usual paraphernalia, such as a St. Andrew's Cross, spanking benches, and a suspension station, it didn't seem half as frightening as she was used to. Brooke peered excitedly into the main room from where they stood, waiting.

"Good evening, Stella, it's nice to have you home." A large, handsome man in leathers and a black, tight-fitting tee met them in the foyer. They sure seemed to breed them big around here.

"Thank you, Ty. I've brought along a guest tonight. This is Brooke Adams; she's staying at the hotel for a few days."

Ty cocked an interested eyebrow at Brooke and gave her a dazzling smile. He looked even more handsome than before. "Good to meet you, Brooke." He shook her hand while Stella signed her in. "May I take your coat and shoes?"

Brooke reeled in surprise before removing her coat. Back in Chicago, that sort of job would never be undertaken by the owner of the club. It would be deemed too menial for them to bother with.

Ty whistled his approval at their outfits. Brooke felt really good in her new dress, and Stella had worn the new red corset with a black skirt.

"I have to give you this," he explained, handing her a sheet of club rules. "I'm sure Stella will keep you in check anyhow, but it's company procedure." He winked as she took it. He really was a charismatic guy.

"Brooke's only planning to take a look around tonight, Ty. She's been to clubs before in Chicago," Stella clarified, handing the pen to Brooke so she could sign her name.

"Well, I'll be around all night if you have any questions Stella can't answer for you. And if you should decide to play later on, be sure to give me a holler. I promise to go easy on you." Ty gave her a wink, making Brooke blush.

They could hear the music from the lobby. Not the usual Nine Inch Nails, which used to give her the creeps as soon as she set foot inside her local Chicago club. This was something she hadn't heard before—sexy, but not scary. Stella led her into the large room, where she was immediately met by smiling faces and welcoming nods. Brooke felt strangely at home already. A small, circular bar was set up in the middle of the room where most of the men seemed to congregate. There were comfy sofas and artificial plants in one corner, while the stations covered the other three walls. It was quite early, so the place wasn't too busy, and the people at the stations were mainly discussing their plans for tonight's scenes.

"Let's get a drink first." Stella led her over to the bar, and the men stood back to let them through. Everyone seemed to know Stella, and seemed genuinely happy to have her back home. Brooke smiled. It must be lovely to have friends who cared about you so much.

"Evening, Ben." Stella caught the eye of the barman who came over and offered them both a beaming smile.

"Stella. Lovely to see you, ma'am, but did you really have to bring this awful weather with you?" His bright blue eyes flashed as he teased her, and everyone around them laughed.

Stella rolled her eyes with a giggle. "There'll be a storm in here tonight if you don't get on and fetch me my usual," she admonished with a laugh.

Ben jumped to it in mock concern and started pouring her a large glass of white wine.

"If you're playing, you're only allowed a couple of alcoholic drinks, but if you're not, you can drink as much as you like. What will you have, Brooke?" Stella smiled at her.

"I'll just have a Coke, please." She thought about

how tired she had been after the champagne last night and decided not to chance alcohol again tonight.

"Coming right up." Ben wasted no time in lining their drinks up on the polished oak bar for them.

"Hey, Brooke, Aunt Stella." Hal Jones squeezed in beside Brooke, grinning broadly at them. Brooke had to look twice to recognize him. Hal looked totally gorgeous in black leather pants and a smart black shirt.

"Hi, Hal." She gasped.

He looked her up and down admiringly. "Love the outfit. Have you been to these places before?"

"Yes, though not quite like this one," Brooke said with a grin. Not only did she have the new dress, but she had put on her makeup and pinned her hair in a sort of half-up, half-down style, which showed off her curls and the length beautifully while keeping it out of her eyes.

Hal chuckled. "No one does BDSM quite like Moone."

"You can say that again." Fred Hammond appeared at the other side of Stella. Ben must have seen him coming because he handed him and Hal a large glass of Coke at the same time.

"Mr. Hammond, how's Blackie?" Brooke's voice was laced with concern for the poor horse.

"Don't you worry about him, he's fine, darlin'. How are you? Travis told me he found you in a ditch." Fred frowned at her.

"I'm fine now, thank you, sir. I bumped my head and got a few more bruises but nothing serious." Brooke looked around. Fred still wore his Stetson and cowboy boots with his Levis, but tonight he wore a smart shirt instead of the checkered ones he had always worn at the stables.

"You come back anytime you feel like a ride, darlin'. No charge, it's the least I can do," Fred offered with a relieved expression.

Brooke beamed at him. "Thank you so much, sir. But I'll be happy to pay…"

"Nonsense. As soon as you're up to it, d'ya hear?" Fred sounded quite gruff and firm about it, so Brooke decided it was best not to argue. She had already had a hard time trying to convince Stella that she should pay for her own dress earlier. She'd have to come up with a way she could repay these nice people later.

"Thank you, sir, I'd like that," she replied meekly, giving him a shy smile.

Fred Hammond seemed happy with that.

"What do you think of the place, then?" Stella asked Brooke, gesturing to the room.

"I like it. Does it get very busy?" Brooke replied, before taking a sip of her coke.

"At weekends mostly. During the week it's pretty quiet."

Just then a woman screamed from the St. Andrew's Cross, and Brooke shot around. Melinda was tied up there, her back to the room. An older man in black leathers and no shirt was using a flogger on her.

"Don't worry about her, she's all noise," Stella said,

shaking her head. Brooke's strong reaction to Melinda's passion seemed to have unnerved her.

"She loves that flogger too," Hal said, turning back to his drink.

Brooke was looking around the room intently. "Where are the dungeon monitors?" she asked.

Fred laughed. "We don't need them here. The sheriff or deputy is in most nights, and we guys all keep our eyes and ears open. We'd all spot trouble a mile off, not that we ever really get any."

"Have you met Mason Bains, our sheriff?" Stella asked Brooke.

She shook her head, causing her blonde curls to fall forward on her shoulders. "No, I haven't met the sheriff or deputy yet."

Stella and the guys exchanged a puzzled look.

Things soon started to heat up in the club, and the sounds of moans and cries could be heard over the music. Every now and then, a loud yelp or scream would cause Brooke to jerk around in her seat, but she was pretty sure nothing bad was going on.

"You want to take a look around?" Stella asked after they had finished their drinks.

Brooke swallowed hard, but smiled. "Sure."

"Perhaps I could show you?" A familiar voice behind her made the hairs at the back of Brooke's neck stand up on end.

She closed her eyes momentarily and then stared at the counter in front of her, not daring to turn around.

Excitement, dread, and anxiety mixed in her stomach, and she thought for a second that she was about to be sick. She took a deep breath and smelled Armani and leather.

"Fine by me. I'll have another glass of wine please, Ben."

It would appear that Stella had decided for her, and Brooke did her best to smile as she eventually turned around. Travis was wearing black leathers and boots, and a black blouson shirt that was open almost to his navel, allowing the hairs of his chest to peek through. To say he looked gorgeous would be a gross understatement!

His eyes seemed to widen and darken as he stared at her.

Brooke watched as Travis gazed over the swell of her voluptuous bosom and down the laces cinching her plump waist. He looked as though he wanted to devour her. His expression turned from hopeful to sultry in an instant, causing her stomach to flip. He held out a hand to her, and she purred as she took it.

"Hi, gorgeous," he murmured and kissed the top of her head.

Brooke flushed and followed him away from the bar. She knew she should be annoyed with him for taking her away from her friends, and she still felt hurt he had betrayed her by peeking at her body without her consent, but it was hard to be angry with someone who radiated this much sex appeal and heat. She took a deep breath and reminded herself of how sexy she had found Chad just before he turned on her, and resolved not to be taken in by it.

"How much have you seen?" Travis was obviously referring to the club, but Brooke had a point to make.

"Not as much as you, obviously," she replied curtly.

His eyes fell and he sighed sadly. She felt sorry for him and almost regretted being so brutal.

"I'm sorry, Brooke. I didn't mean to—"

"Was it while I was unconscious or when I took a shower?" she snapped at him.

He turned to face her, running a frustrated hand through his tousled waves. He still held her hand. "The shower. It wasn't intentional. I opened the window in the bedroom and caught your reflection in the closet mirror."

She took a deep breath. It didn't make it right, but she was relieved he hadn't just peered around the corner like some cheap voyeur.

"My body's private," she informed him simply.

"I know, darlin'. I'm so sorry." He placed a finger under her chin, which tilted her face up to look at him.

Her stomach flipped again. He really was the most handsome man she had ever seen, and she had to fight hard to keep her resolve not to kiss him there and then.

"Why didn't you tell *me* instead of telling Kent about my body?" She jutted out her chin and concentrated on the betrayal instead of how sexy he looked.

"I didn't know how to tell you without scaring you. I didn't want you to think I'd been spying on you."

"You had."

"I didn't mean to, darlin', I swear."

"So why brag to Kent about it, then?" Her eyes were steely as she spat the words out, forcing herself to dwell on the hurt and deception instead of what she really wanted to concentrate on—what those lips would feel like all over her body.

"I was worried about you. I could see you've been hurt, and I was hoping we could help you."

"You can't!" She flared at him as tears threatened the corners of her eyes.

"How do you know?"

"It's none of your business."

His grip on her arm tightened as she tried to turn away.

"OK, I'm sorry. We just care about you, that's all." His voice was calm and quiet, infuriating her all the more. She hadn't shouted yet, but she sure felt like yelling at him. Her blood boiled, and her face turned red with frustration and anger.

She stared at his too-handsome face and wanted to slap the concerned expression from it. "I don't need you to care about me," she hissed, glaring defiantly at him.

Brooke expected him to apologize once again and geared herself up to deal with the hangdog expression she assumed would grace his gorgeous face. She was wrong. Travis's eyebrow cocked up and he stared into her fuming face.

"Really?" he asked in an even voice.

Brooke started to tremble. She wasn't sure if he was about to walk away from her for good. Dread filled her entire body, and she wondered if she had pushed him too far. After all, he had apologized, and his reasoning did sound plausible. He didn't seem like the kind of guy who would peep at a girl in the shower, either. With his looks, he didn't need to resort to dirty tricks.

She sighed, forcing herself to look away from him. She couldn't deny that the thought of being cared for by the two gorgeous hunks would be a dream come true, but she knew she was in no position to stick around playing happy families. Much as she would love to stay, she was on her way out of there just as soon as Mother Nature allowed it. Chad would be gaining on her even if he couldn't actually get into town yet; the floods wouldn't last forever.

She looked back up at him, nodding sadly. "I can look after myself. Besides, I'm leaving tomorrow. I can get Stella to show me around the club tonight." She turned to walk away from him, but he held her firm.

"I said *I'll* show you the club." His voice was low and deep.

Something about that voice had an unholy effect on her.

Travis's demeanor changed in an instant. He stood tall and determined. He was apparently done with apologizing. "I know this place isn't your typical BDSM club, but then Moone isn't a typical county town. Folk here have different views on life. We tend to live and let live.

So long as no one gets hurt, we can all live the way we want to. The same goes for their kinks. We don't practice the high protocol you might be used to. We come here to have fun, not to get terrified or harmed."

Brooke's stomach churned as he spoke. He was like a tour guide in one respect, telling her all the facts. On the other hand, he was obviously getting across a few very personal points. She followed him over to the spanking bench, where a very pretty sub was enjoying a pleasurable session with her attentive Dom. She seemed petite with short, dark hair that fell over her face. She was naked and moaned with pleasure at each whack and rub. If she wasn't already in subspace, she wasn't far from it. Brooke's pussy gushed as she imagined Travis doing that to her. She squeezed her thighs together, clenching herself. When she looked up, she flushed to see that Travis had been studying her reaction to the scene. A sly smirk crossed his face.

"Have you ever been spanked?" His question was reasonable under the circumstances, but Brooke felt too annoyed to answer him.

"That's *my* business," she replied curtly.

He sighed and led her to another station. A female sub was tied to a sort of bed while her Dom poured melted wax onto her breasts. Brooke had seen this done before, and wasn't surprised to hear the gasps and groans of the young sub, who appeared to be in a dreamy state.

"Knife play?" Travis asked before leading her to another station.

Brooke shook her head, her mouth turning dry.

"Threesome?" He was studying her face intently.

She shrugged. She was darned if she was going to tell him how excited she was at the prospect, but he could read her like a book.

An oversized bed stood in one corner, and a middle-aged lady was enjoying some double penetration from a couple of younger men. She was screeching her delight as they pounded rhythmically into her, grunting with each thrust. Brooke studied the woman's face. She had expected her to have a pained expression, as Brooke had experienced anal sex before—though not entirely through choice—and found it hurt far more than she expected. The woman obviously relished the sensations, as she cried out for more, harder thrusts. The men were murmuring to her, and stroking her arms and back as well as her breasts. Brooke had never seen so much affection and was astonished at the effect it had on her. Her face flushed and tears pricked the corners of her eyes. Blinking hurriedly, she looked away in case Travis caught her expression.

Too late. He grinned but didn't speak. The three on the bed reached their climax simultaneously, and the roars and screams were tremendous. Brooke's pussy clenched with excitement and she couldn't stop herself imagining how that would feel if Travis and Kent were doing that to her.

As they walked away from the bed, she heard a loud gasp from the St. Andrew's Cross, where a different couple was now playing. Brooke's eyes darted around and fixated on the woman tied with her back to the room. She was much rounder than Melinda. She groaned and leaned into the wooden structure. Her face, which leaned sideways against the cross, looked serene and blissful.

Brooke slowly made her way over to take a closer look. Travis followed, giving her some space. Brooke's eyes were still fixated on the woman, judging her reactions. After a while, she examined the whip in use. It was a single tail. She gulped, but kept her nerve. The Dom was placing the strokes evenly over the woman's body and was evidently at expert at analyzing her reactions, as he seemed to be giving her exactly what she needed. The Dom had his back to Brooke, and it was hard to see him properly in the shadows. He had wavy, fair hair and wore leathers with no shirt. She saw the ripples of his shoulders and back as he wielded the whip, and suddenly her mouth fell open. So this was what it was supposed to be like.

Travis took a step closer to Brooke.

After a while, Brooke gazed up at him. Travis motioned for her to look a little closer.

It was Kent! His strokes were perfect, every one precisely positioned. He read his sub's reactions well and adjusted the severity accordingly. The woman didn't appear to be a pain slut, but she enjoyed the intensity she received, judging by her contented moans. Brooke had to admit that Kent was good at his job. Stella had been right about him being a perfectionist. She walked over to the side of the scene area to study Kent's face. It was beautiful. She was amazed to see his serene expression and calm demeanor.

She had never seen a person in Dom space before but had read about it. This must be what it looked like. Kent's gorgeous face was concentrating on the woman in front of him. He didn't scowl or grimace as Chad always had. He didn't yell at the woman as he whipped her. He was perfectly composed and in control of himself and his actions. Brooke had never seen anything so peaceful. She could see his lips moving as he spoke soothingly to his sub, occasionally walking right up to her to stroke her skin with his soft hands and murmur in her ear. Brooke guessed he was checking she was OK before continuing. She marveled at how caring Kent was with the woman, and felt a twinge of jealousy.

"You OK?" Travis's soft voice pulled her from her thoughts.

Brooke stared up at him and was surprised that he appeared all blurry. She wiped her eyes hurriedly. Travis's gorgeous face smiled kindly at her. Brooke's stomach lurched as he reached down and cupped her face in his strong hands. She stared into those deep, dark eyes as he nibbled at her lips before engulfing her mouth in a soft, sensual kiss. Her whole body softened, and she had to cling on to his arms to stop herself from melting into a puddle on the floor. Travis's kiss was soft and loving, and she couldn't get enough of it. Brooke wanted it to last forever. A burn ignited in her stomach and coursed through her veins. She kissed him back, slowly at first, but then passion overtook her and she devoured his mouth deliriously.

Travis's hands left her face and wrapped around her voluptuous frame. He breathed in her scent. Everything around them seemed to disappear, and Brooke let him lose himself in the moment, in her.

Chapter Eight

Kent looked after his little sub until she was ready to join her friends at the bar. He had taken her to one of the sofas, only to find that Travis and Brooke were sitting on one at the far end. Brooke sat in Travis's lap, and they were gazing at each other and kissing lovingly. Kent was relieved she hadn't bolted as soon as she'd seen either of them. He knew they were taking a risk by arranging for her to see him in action, but thought it best to show her exactly what he did with a single tail whip. His heart leapt at the sight of them giving each other lingering kisses and longing looks, and ached to join in.

Travis beckoned Kent over once his sub had left, and he cautiously went across to sit with them. "Are you OK?" he asked Brooke softly.

She flushed when she saw him and nodded.

"I'm so sorry about everything," he said gently.

She shook her head. "It wasn't your fault. I was just a bit scared, that's all. I shouldn't have made a fuss." She smiled weakly at him, and he sat forward, studying her.

"Scared of what?" He saw her tense up as soon as he asked but thought it was probably the best time to find out. Especially now that he knew she wasn't who she said she was. Mason had come through with some interesting information this afternoon.

Brooke sat up straight on Travis's lap.

"When you see someone waving a whip around, I think most people would be afraid of being hit." She tried to sound light and cheery.

"Why would you think that? I wasn't even near you, let alone facing you." He stared at her face and noticed it tense and twitch nervously as she fought to find an answer.

Brooke squeezed her lips together, fuming. "I'm sorry. I got it wrong, OK?" she bit the words out.

Travis sighed.

Brooke looked back to Travis with a forced smile. "I need to get back to Stella. I don't want her to think I'm being rude by neglecting her."

Travis chanced a quick kiss to her head. Nothing like the kisses they had been enjoying when Kent came over.

"Thank you for showing me around tonight, Travis. Goodnight, Kent." Her voice was cool as she got up and left them.

"What the hell did you do that for?" Travis hissed at Kent once she was out of earshot.

"I was hoping she might confide in us about what had frightened her. She seemed all relaxed and happy. I thought it was the right time," Kent replied ruefully.

"It was the right time for you to stop interrogating her and start kissing her. I had her all warmed up nice. Now we're right back to square one!" Travis was clearly pissed.

"I'm sorry," Kent said with a sigh. "I misread the situation."

Travis ran a hand through his dark hair and snuggled closer to his partner. "We'll have to figure something out," he reassured him.

"I don't think she likes me." Kent pouted. "I always seem to fuck up when she's around."

"You don't know shit." Travis snorted. "You should have seen her face when she was watching you tonight. She more than likes you, buddy, believe me. You just need to stop working for a while and start relaxing. All the questions are making her edgy."

Kent nuzzled back against Travis.

"I just need to know what the hell's going on with her, you know? She's given us a false name, she's covered in welts and scars, and she's scared to death of something. If we don't find out soon, she's gonna disappear, I just know it. Every time I look at her, I can see she's on the brink of running. I wanna know what she's running *from*." Kent's chin stiffened as he spoke.

Travis stroked Kent's hand. "I know, bud. I wanna know too, but she won't tell us until she's ready. Besides, we don't know she's given us a false name. She could have just borrowed the car."

Kent shook his head. "No, Brooke Anderson is too close to Brooke Adams to be a coincidence, bro. She's given us a false name, all right. Mason's going to run a check on Brooke Anderson, see what he can come up with."

"Well he'd better be quick. She's planning on leaving town tomorrow," Travis said, looking over at Brooke sitting on a bar stool chatting with Stella and Hal. They'd been joined by the local billionaire, Rich Buchanan, as well as Don Montgomery.

Kent stiffened. "She can't."

"She can if this rain holds off. By my reckoning, the road'll be passable by the morning if it doesn't start again tonight." He sighed miserably, watching Brooke and Stella say their good-byes and head for the door. "I don't know about you, buddy, but I could use a drink."

Don and Hal were walking the women home, but Rich was still sat at the bar grinning like a Cheshire cat.

"Couple of beers please, Ben," Travis ordered as he took the stool next to Rich.

Kent slumped onto the stool beside his partner's, deep in thought.

"You look pleased with yourself," Travis said to Rich as he took his drink.

"I am. Guess who's got a hot date for The Brandon Boys gig tomorrow night?" Rich's dimples showed as he grinned. His handsome face lit up.

"Go on then, what poor, unsuspecting fool have you got lined up to disappoint this time?" Kent teased as he swigged his beer.

"Brooke Adams. She's new in town, staying at the Montgomery."

Travis's face turned to thunder and he stood up angrily.

Kent stood up too, placing a warning hand on his partner's arm.

"What in hell do you think you're playing at, Rich Buchanan? Didn't you see her with *me* tonight?" Travis spoke through gritted teeth, and several people looked over to see the commotion.

Rich arrogantly took a large glug of his beer before turning back to Travis. "I saw you. I also saw her leave *without* you. Seems to me she's not tied to anyone— much less you." He resumed drinking his beer.

"Leave it, bro," Kent warned. "Come on, let's go."

Travis clenched his fist and scowled as Kent led him out of the building.

Brooke had a troubled night. Her emotions were in turmoil. She was also aware that the rain had stopped and the road could be clear today. She really had to think about leaving town before Chad found her.

She took a deep breath and headed for the shower. Her bathroom window was open, and she could hear the birds chirping outside. It looked as though the sun might be shining later. As she washed, she couldn't help but start to feel optimistic.

She had a date tonight, a guy she'd only just met. He was handsome and charming and witty. He seemed really nice, and she was sure she'd have fun with him. He didn't seem at all intense and was well aware that she was leaving town any day now, so there was no chance of anything lasting. It would be fun to go out with someone without complications. Especially as they were going to see The Brandon Boys, a local country band. She started to hum a Dolly Parton song as she showered and dressed.

"Good morning, sweetie." Stella arrived downstairs at the same time as Brooke. Don had already eaten and begun his duties behind the reception desk, so the ladies ate together.

Brooke helped herself to a glass of juice from the breakfast bar before taking a seat opposite Stella. She was wearing jeans and a pretty top today. Stella wore slacks and a loose-fitting shirt.

"Thank you so much for last night," Brooke said with a beaming smile.

Stella beamed back. "You're welcome. I'm really glad you enjoyed yourself."

Zak arrived with their toast and coffee and Stella poured. She looked at Brooke a little quizzically. "You like Travis and Kent, don't you, dear?"

Brooke blushed. She knew exactly what Stella was thinking. *So why are you going out with Rich tonight?* She steeled herself before flashing another big smile at her friend.

"Yes, they're really nice guys." She took a bite of her toast.

Stella frowned. She was probably considering how to ask the question without sounding offensive.

"It's a pity neither of them asked me to see The Brandon Boys tonight, really." Brooke put them both out of their misery, "I guess they're busy or maybe it's not their thing. Or they could be going with someone else." She shrugged, trying to sound disinterested.

Stella took a sip of her coffee, studying Brooke carefully. Brooke resumed her breakfast.

Zak arrived with extra toast. They were the only ones in the restaurant again today.

"I need to help Don with some paperwork later," Stella said. "What are your plans for today?"

Brooke tucked in to another slice of toast. "I thought I'd take a walk. I need to check out the roads. They might be passable by now."

"Are you in a hurry to leave us?" Stella sounded a little sad.

"I'll be sorry to leave you and my friends here, but I

really need to get going. I've got to get back to work," Brooke said with a sincere smile.

"Of course." Stella smiled back.

They finished their breakfast and Brooke went upstairs to get ready. She could hear Don on the phone when she came back down. He was frowning and sounded as though he was dealing with a very awkward customer. Brooke was glad. It meant she didn't need to speak to him on her way out. Don could be so intense.

It was a clear, fresh day outside. Brooke shivered and pulled on the sweater she had grabbed for her walk. She headed out of town and found the roads had dried up quite a bit since yesterday. The cool air washed over her and she sighed. It looked as though she could drive on now.

Chad would be so pissed with her that he was coming after her to *make* her sign that stupid thing. What if he had seen her drive off and followed her? He could be just outside town now, waiting for the roads to clear so he could get here and start asking around. She wouldn't be hard to find in a place like this. She scowled when she saw that the road into town seemed to be quite drivable. There were a few quite large puddles, but nothing a decent car wouldn't be able to handle. Unfortunately, Chad drove a *very* decent car. Not like her old banger.

Brooke sighed and turned back for town. She had made a commitment to go to the gig with Rich tonight but would definitely leave first thing tomorrow morning.

Kent thumped the desk of his small home office. He had just spoken to Mason Bains. That, on top of the call he had received first thing this morning from Don Montgomery, was about as much as he could handle.

"Travis, you anywhere near the house, bro?" He spoke into the radio as he went to look out the window.

"Just in the stables. You want me to come back, buddy?"

"Yup. I'll have a coffee ready." Kent switched off the device and went to the kitchen. The coffeepot was on all day when he was working from home, and today was no exception.

"Something else?" Travis strolled into the kitchen a few minutes later, a worried frown on his face. He put an arm around Kent and kissed his cheek before taking the cup from him. They sat at the little round table at one end of the kitchen.

"I told Mason about the call we got from Don Montgomery. He agrees that Don was right to worry. Now Don said the guy who called him was asking about a Brooke Anderson. Don obviously told him no one by that name had passed through town. Mason just told me that Shane Bowman at the food store had a call from someone asking the same thing." Kent sighed.

"Did Shane tell him anything?" They both knew Brooke was bound to have visited the local store at some point during the last few days.

Kent shook his head. "No, Shane didn't like the sound of the guy. Said he was asking too many questions, real persistent-like. He told him the town's been cut off for days and no one's been through this way in quite a while."

"Did he buy it?"

"I sure hope so. Shane called Mason right away just in case it was important."

"Hallelujah for that." Travis took a long swig of his coffee.

"There's something else." Kent frowned. "You know Brooke said she worked for a manufacturing company, something to do with tires Stella said? Well, Mason checked out all the large rubber companies in Chicago and Brooke Anderson did work at one of them, Robertson's Rubber, up until six months ago."

"Why did she leave?" Travis stared at his partner across the table.

Kent shook his head. "They don't know. Mason spoke to the manager, who said Brooke was a good little worker. She was there a few years and seemed really happy most of the time. She was very popular with all the staff, really helpful at work, and liked to socialize with them afterward. He said that a few months before she left, she gradually stopped going out with them and became quite withdrawn. She lost her bubbly personality. Brooke started taking time off too. He guessed it was something to do with the guy she was seeing but didn't know his name. Just said he drove a blue sports car—real expensive-looking."

"Unlike Brooke's clapped-out old banger," Travis seethed.

"Yeah. Anyway, about six months ago she stopped turning in for work. After a few days, she rang her boss and told him she had to go away and wouldn't be working for them anymore. The guy said she was in tears on the phone. He couldn't get it out of her where she was going or why, but he said something didn't feel right somehow. He asked around her friends but no one knew anything. One of her girlfriends went around to her apartment a few times but never got an answer. They guessed she'd left town, like she said."

Travis took a slow sip of his coffee. "D'you reckon she's been on the road all this time?"

"Chicago's a long way off. She wouldn't have driven all this way for a few days' vacation." Kent frowned.

"Do we know where the boyfriend is?"

"Not yet. Mason's looking into that. Hasn't come up with a name yet, but he will."

"Probably explains who she's running from. If he's the fucker that did all that to her body, I can't wait to meet him myself." Travis scowled.

"Join the line, bro," Kent fumed, shaking his head.

"Looks like the weather's improved. The road must be passable by now. If the bastard's on to her, he could show up here anytime."

"That's what I thought. I think we'd best be going to that gig tonight just to keep an eye on things."

"You don't think I was planning to leave her alone with Rich the Red-Light Wrangler, do you?"

Kent chuckled. "Not really."

Rich had a real bad reputation locally for being a bit of a manwhore. He was also a bit of an enigma; the folks in town took him to be bisexual, but he was known to only take women home with him. His daddy didn't approve of gays, apparently, particularly not in his own family.

The phone rang again and Kent rushed over to answer it. His gorgeous face turned to a puzzled frown.

"OK, boss, thanks for letting me know. Can you send it here as soon as you get it? Much obliged. Keep me posted." He sat back down, a thoughtful expression on his face.

"Mason?"

Kent nodded gravely. "Someone he knows at the police department in Chicago recognized the name. Mason said the guy can't recall the exact circumstances, but he thinks someone in his department has been trying to get hold of a Brooke Anderson to find out why she failed to appear in court last week. He's going to check it out and let us know. He's also agreed to forward a picture of her so we can check it's the same girl."

Travis ran his hand through his hair. "Well at least it's something," he said with a sigh. He frowned at Kent's unhappy face. "You think she's done something wrong?"

Kent shook his head. "I don't know. It's not only criminals that wind up in court."

Travis grabbed his partner's arms across the table. "Then what?"

Kent sighed. "Mason said the guy warned him that if this Brooke Anderson is who he thinks she is, the pictures ain't pretty."

Chapter Nine

Brooke hummed a country song as she prepared for her date. She couldn't remember the last time a guy took her out. A pang of sadness hit her that she wasn't going with Travis and Kent, though. Travis had mentioned the gig when they were up at the ranch but hadn't said anything about it last night, so she assumed he'd either forgotten or changed his mind. She felt a warm glow in her stomach as she remembered Travis's kisses from last night. For a while there, everything seemed to be right with the world. She'd even managed to forget all about Chad while she was in Travis's arms.

Her thoughts turned to Kent. He had been so gorgeous when he was using the single tail on the sub; Brooke wondered what it must have felt like. She knew only too well how it felt when Chad whipped her, but he had always been angry with her. The sub Kent was with was obviously enjoying the sensations. Kent had seemed to be entranced by the whole scene, although he was very much in control of everything in it.

There was tranquility about both Kent and his sub that Brooke couldn't get over. Kent was so handsome too. At one point she had hoped to be kissed by him last night as well as Travis. Brooke sighed. It seemed a pity that whenever things looked as though they were going well, it always ended up getting spoiled.

She left her long blonde waves loose and wore her best black jeans with a very pretty top. It was black and had a low drawstring at the front. The material felt like satin, and it had green-and-purple floral embroidery around the edges. The sleeves were wide and felt luxurious against her skin. It had a handkerchief hem that hung just low enough to drape over her curves. Her makeup was a little heavier than her normal natural look, and she felt good about herself.

After pulling on her boots, Brooke delved into her backpack for her small purse. It was made of plain black leather and blended well with any of her outfits. Something caught her eye and she bit her lip as she checked it. The outside pocket of her backpack was very worn. She slid her hand inside and felt what she was looking for— the statement. She didn't know why she still had it with her. It was going to be evidence she had planned to show the police. She wanted to prove to them that Chad was still local and was trying to force her to sign the false declaration to get himself off the hook. Too late now. She stuffed it back into the pocket and hid the bag under the bed before leaving the room.

"I was just going to call you." Don Montgomery was standing at the reception desk when she reached the foyer. "Your date's just arrived."

"Hi." Rich Buchanan looked scrumptious in his designer jeans and white shirt. It wasn't just any shirt, though; this was pure white and had scroll embroidery creating a yoke effect around his muscular shoulders. It looked as though it might be made of silk or something similar, and it had a luxurious sheen, which glistened when the light caught it. He wore polished tan boots and a matching hat and had a suede jacket hooked around his finger, which was perched just by his shoulder. He was leaning casually against the wall, waiting for her.

Brooke's mouth went dry, and she was suddenly aware that she was gawping at him.

"Hi, Rich," she managed at last.

He grinned. It wasn't the kind of grin she was used to from Travis; this was a self-satisfied smirk. Brooke suddenly felt a little irritated by his arrogance. He obviously knew he was handsome and looked pleased that she had noticed it too. She took a deep breath as he held the door open for her to leave. "You look lovely tonight," he murmured as she brushed past him.

"Thank you, so do you," she replied and then immediately regretted her words when she saw his smug expression.

"I've brought my car, as you can see." Rich gestured to the top-of-the-range sports car that he had parked directly outside the front door of the hotel. Its cobalt-blue metallic finish gleamed in the twilight. Even the hubcaps glinted bright silver in the light. She wondered how come his car managed to look so immaculate when everyone else's was always covered in dust and dirt. He probably employed someone to do nothing but keep his car clean. Brooke seethed a little at his audacity.

"We can walk from here, it's only the end of the road," Brooke replied with a frown.

"Or we could arrive in style." His smug titter made her grimace.

"I'd much rather get some fresh air, and it's not raining right now. Do you mind if we walk?"

As Brooke was speaking, he unlocked the car and was about to open the door for her to get in. He sighed irritably. This guy was obviously not used to a woman not complying with his auspicious plans. An angry glint crossed his eyes and Brooke flinched. It was only for a fraction of a second, and then he seemed unperturbed again, but Brooke knew better than to ignore it.

"Very well," he said with an exasperated flounce and locked the car again.

It was just as well really, as Brooke had already walked past him and his beloved vehicle and was on her way down the drive. He caught up with her within a few strides and casually slung his arm around her shoulder. Although she tensed, she thought better than to argue with him, so she said nothing.

"What brought you to Moone?" he asked nonchalantly.

"I had a few days vacation and fancied some peace and quiet. Do you live near here?" Brooke was becoming an expert at fending off questions and knew this guy would be much happier talking about himself than anything else.

He chuckled incredulously. "Don't you know where I live?"

She frowned. "No. Why would I know that?"

They were on the main street now. He gestured to the mountain behind them. "At the foot of that mountain, to the west, is the Buchanan Ranch." He sounded like a tour guide, and she rolled her eyes.

"Is it very big?" She could guess the answer but thought it best to indulge him as he was clearly dying to tell her.

He sniggered. "Quite big, sweetheart." His voice was patronizing and she wanted to kick him. She refrained, but only just.

"I presume it's your family's place, then? Do you live at home?" She asked as sweetly as she could, but could tell by his expression that she had hit a raw nerve.

"It's the family ranch but I kind of run it. I live on my own. I've got a shack on the estate. I might take you back there later if you're a good girl." He squeezed her tighter, and she thought she was about to vomit.

"Do you ride, Brooke? We've got loads of horses. I've got a free hour tomorrow afternoon actually. Maybe I could take you out?"

"I do ride, but I'm heading home tomorrow. Thank you anyway." She smiled sweetly at him.

"Well if things go well tonight, I might just tempt you to stay a little longer." He sounded snide, which made her skin crawl.

"Sorry, cowboy, I've got work to get back to."

He snorted. "What do you do? Work in a shop?"

She cringed. He obviously had her taped as the "little woman" and anything she said would only give him more ammunition to condescend her with. She thought it best to say nothing and just smiled.

Brooke was still trying to imagine what is was about the supercilious ass that made her think a date with him would actually be fun, when they arrived at the bar.

He led her in and found a table for her to sit at near the front of the stage. To his credit, he was a perfect gentleman and held the chair out for her to sit down before heading for the bar to fetch their drinks.

It was a small, friendly bar with wooden floors and a tiny stage against one wall. A large area had been left bare toward one side of the stage, and several people were already dancing along to an Alan Jackson song being played while the band set up.

Brooke smiled at the vast array of outfits they wore.

Some of the girls wore dresses or flared skirts while others preferred jeans. Some of them had vest-tops on while others wore shirts or pretty tops. The guys were all in jeans, most of them really smart ones. They mostly wore shirts, although one or two wore T-shirts, showing off their bulging biceps. Quite a few people wore cowboy hats, and certainly looked the part with their thumbs tucked into their belts while they line danced across the floor.

This was the sort of place Brooke loved. All the tables looked very old and quite shabby, and all the chairs were odd. It had a homey feel about it. It smelled of wood and beer. Some people were sitting around or standing at the bar chatting excitedly. She recognized Hal at the bar and gave him a wave. He beamed when he saw her. There was no sign of Travis or Kent though, and she felt a little pang of disappointment.

Brooke watched the band set up the last of their equipment. There were four good-looking guys, obviously brothers. She could tell straight away which one was going to be the lead singer—he was already flirting with the girls as he straightened his mic and tidied the leads across the stage. Brooke smirked.

"Here you go," Rich placed a wineglass in front of her and she sat forward. He poured her a drink and placed the bottle on the table. He was drinking a pint, which he'd already half finished. "What're you smiling at?" He glanced over toward the stage, but evidently couldn't see anything comical there.

"Thank you. Oh, it's nothing really, just some girls eyeing up the band."

"There's something about being in a band which seems to have the girls flocking, isn't there? I can't see why myself. I usually find people who go around playing a guitar for money never seem to have any."

Brooke shook her head and sighed.

The band started up as the lights dimmed, and everyone cheered. Big spotlights swooped across the stage, picking out the hunky Brandon Boys.

Brooke was grateful for the distraction, as she was already bored with Rich's choice of conversation. She tapped her foot in time to the music and found her mood lightening by the minute. Her date seemed to be enjoying himself too. She saw a good-looking guy come up to Rich, place another pint in front of him, and whisper something into his ear. Rich beamed and flushed slightly. Then the man walked away grinning and Rich went back to watching the band.

"Shall we dance?" Rich was on his feet as a catchy tune started up and Brooke stared up at him in surprise. She hadn't taken him for a dancer.

She smiled and sprang to her feet. She couldn't remember the last time she'd danced. He led her to the busy dance floor and twirled her around. There were several other people on the floor, and the atmosphere was electric. Those who were sitting down were clapping in time and singing along, and the band was really great.

During a couples dance, one of the guitarists looked

over at Brooke and winked. Rich automatically took her in his arms and danced close to her. Brooke flushed. She didn't see Rich as her type at all, but he sure had a jealous streak.

They stayed on the dance floor most of the night after that. She decided Rich was loads of fun as long as you weren't trying to make conversation with him.

"Mind if I cut in?"

A deep voice Brooke knew well growled from behind her and her pussy clenched. Rich stepped back, letting go of his date.

"Just this once," he replied sulkily and nodded to Brooke.

Travis grabbed her from behind and swung her around to face him. Her heart leapt. He looked amazing. He wore a smart turquoise shirt that had the sleeves rolled back, revealing a brown, tan, and turquoise contrasting pattern, which was also featured under the placket and collar. He teamed it with smart black jeans and pointed-toe boots. He smelled divine—Armani was obviously his favorite scent, and it suited him. Brooke placed her hands on his shoulders as the music slowed down. His shirt felt like satin under her trembling hands. His stubble brushed her forehead, and she felt his heat as he pulled her close.

"Having fun, darlin'?" His voice was a deep murmur in her ear, and it did wonderful things to her.

"I am now," she whispered.

He chuckled deep in his throat, and she felt it reverberate through his ripped chest. He had left half his buttons undone, allowing his chest hair to poke through. Brooke loved that look on him.

"It looked to me like you were getting along fine," Travis said with a smile.

Brooke looked over to where Rich was strolling toward the door of the bathroom.

"He's OK, but he's not you," she confessed.

Travis's hot mouth reached down and devoured hers in a long, sensual kiss. His tongue forced its way into her mouth, taking possession of her. She gasped into his mouth as her pussy gushed and she felt his erection dig into her. She was surrounded by his heat, his scent, and his passion. She grabbed at his hair as they kissed and he squeezed her ass, while his other arm wrapped around her like a boa.

All too soon the music stopped and Rich was back, a whiskey in his hand. He was quietly seething.

"Time to give back my date, Beaumont." Although Rich tried to make it sound like a friendly request, the expression on his face told another story.

Travis slowly pulled away, leaving Brooke feeling bereft. He winked at her and grinned. "See you later, darlin'." He gave her another quick kiss on the top of her head while Rich downed his whiskey and placed his glass on a nearby table.

Brooke smiled back at Travis while Rich slipped his

arms around her. She watched her cowboy make his way back to the bar and noticed Kent waiting there. Kent looked very smart in his dark jeans and pale green Western-style shirt. Brooke sighed at the sight of the two handsome men and allowed her mind to stray momentarily. If only things had worked out differently for the three of them...

"What're you thinking about, sweetheart?" Rich's voice brought her from her reverie, and she gasped when she saw the sinister look on his face. She recognized the expression as one that Chad used to give her when he asked the exact same question. It was a look that said he knew darn well that she wasn't thinking about him and he wanted her to spell it out to him so he could punish her for it. She tensed in his arms and tried to step backward, but he held her tight.

Rich sniggered. "Now how about some of that lip action you were so keen on giving your cowboy over there?" His voice was a sneer as he leaned in to kiss her. He held her so tight she had nowhere to go, and she smelled the whiskey before his mouth assaulted her lips.

Panic flared through her. She suddenly felt as though Chad was right there, and for a moment she thought she could even smell him. Her blood ran cold and prickles raced up her back as horror engulfed her. Rich's mouth attacked hers and she tried to scream. Her hands thumped his arms, trying to loosen his grip. She tried to shake her head to get away from his mouth, but he was too strong. Eventually she did the only thing she could think of. She drew her knee up hard into his balls.

Rich crumpled, letting go of her as if she had the plague. "You bitch! I'll—"

"You'll do nothing, Rich Buchanan, unless you want to spend the night in a cell. Now leave the lady alone."

Tears streamed down Brooke's face and she trembled. Kent wrapped his arms around her and led her away from the dance floor. Travis took hold of Rich and hauled him outside.

Kent led Brooke to a quiet corner of the room and held her while she sobbed, trembling. "I-I didn't want him to..." she stammered.

"I know, baby. It's all right now," he soothed, stroking her hair and kissing the top of her head.

Brooke took deep breaths to steady her nerves while Kent's gorgeous scent enveloped her. His heat surrounded her as his large body swathed her in safety. She found herself relaxing and melted into his chest.

Kent's body felt softer than Travis's, and he smelled slightly sweeter. His smooth hand caressed the side of her face before tilting her chin up to him. His lips slowly drifted down to hers, and she lost herself in his loving kiss. It was the first time Kent had been this intimate with her, and she moaned with delight. His kiss wasn't as forceful as Travis's—he was a gentle lover, and she marveled at how the guys seemed so different and yet so similar. They were halves of a whole. She imagined herself being loved by both of them; they would give her everything she needed and more.

Kent's hands ran through her hair and grazed over her body while they kissed. He nipped at her neck, creating goose bumps up and down her spine. She shuddered and he chuckled. She loved that sound, deep and low. Brooke was suddenly aware how damp she'd become. He didn't notice, just smothered her in soft kisses. She wanted this to go on forever.

Eventually Kent pulled back slowly as someone behind him cleared his throat for the umpteenth time.

"Sorry to interrupt. Travis seems to be having some trouble out there with Buchanan. Do you want me to call the sheriff?"

Kent sighed. "No, I'll deal with it." He reluctantly let go of Brooke and gave her a stunning smile. "You OK now, baby?" His face was beautiful, but concerned was etched in his eyes until she smiled up at him.

"I'm fine, thank you," she whispered.

"I won't be long. You stay here," he replied, giving her another dazzling smile before heading out the door.

Brooke hugged herself as she watched him swagger away from her. He was so gorgeous. She felt a little sorry for him. He always seemed to say the wrong thing and make her mad, and yet she was sure she was falling for him every bit as much as she was falling for Travis. Could a ménage with these guys really work? She had never thought seriously about it before, but it would be perfect if it would. They were so wonderful to her. They made her feel loved and safe, something she had never thought she could be. Travis was such fun and Kent was so gentle. She knew she could love them back. She might already be in love with them.

Her stomach lurched and her heart leapt at the thought. She giggled to herself. She felt scared and excited at the same time. Her thoughts drifted to last night at Ty's. Maybe the guys would take her there. She had always wanted to explore BDSM and knew now that what she had experienced so far was nothing like it. All she had felt until now was pain and fear. She was sure it would be totally different with Kent and Travis. Her mind drifted back to the sight of Travis and Kent in their leathers, and she started getting even wetter.

A loud shout from outside made her jump.

"Don't you worry about them. Jonah's gone to help out. Poor guy doesn't know what he's gotten himself into." Hal was beside her in a flash.

"Is everything OK?" She stared at him, wide-eyed. He seemed to be taking all this in his stride.

"Of course. Those guys can look after themselves, don't you worry about that." He grinned before taking a sip of his beer.

"But someone could get badly hurt."

"Na. Buchanan's been drinking again. He often gets like this."

Brooke frowned. "But he seemed so..."

"Oh he's a nice guy, don't get me wrong. He just can't hold his drink, that's all. He often gets like this when he's had a few. The guys'll probably hit each other a few times and then put him in cell to sleep it off. He won't remember any of it in the morning." Hal grinned.

"Hit each other?"

Brooke rushed over to the door. Travis, Kent, and another man, presumably Jonah, had formed a circle around Rich, who was swaying on his feet. They were a little way off, but she could see that the man she didn't know had blood dripping from his mouth. Brooke gasped. She couldn't see the faces of her cowboys as they both had their backs to her. She just prayed that they were OK.

Kent was ordering Rich around. She loved his domineering voice; he really commanded authority. "You either do this the easy way or the hard way, Buchanan, the choice is yours. Either you come with me now and get yourself some rest, or I'll cuff you and drag you over there. We can leave the cuffs on too, and you know you won't get comfortable all night that way. Now, what's it gonna be, 'cause I ain't got all night?"

"Only 'cause you and lover boy here wanna get with my date," Rich sneered as he slurred his words, and Brooke turned hot with embarrassment.

"She was our girl way before she was your date, and you know it." Travis's voice was deep and gruff.

Brooke liked the sound of being "their girl" and felt a warm glow inside to know they already regarded her as such.

"Then you should've asked her out." Rich turned to point at Travis.

"Yes, we should've, and we would have too if we hadn't gone and forgotten it was tonight," Travis agreed ruefully.

"Don't sweat it, bro. We had a lot going on," Kent reassured him.

With one step forward, Kent quickly snapped a pair of handcuffs onto Rich's wrists.

"Hey!" Rich's head jerked around to berate Kent, but he didn't seem worried.

Where did the cuffs come from? Bemused, and seeing that the situation was now safe, Brooke went out the door and started to make her way toward them.

"You got a problem, Buchanan?" Kent was as cool as a cucumber as he yanked at Rich's arm.

Rich didn't get the chance to reply as the sheriff's big black SUV pulled up just then and a guy jumped out.

"Really? *Again*, Buchanan?" The sheriff shook his head as Kent handed him over.

Rich muttered some profanities as he climbed into the ride seat. It appeared to be a well-rehearsed routine for him.

"Did you get the pictures I sent you?" the sheriff asked Kent as soon as he'd secured their prisoner.

Kent sighed and nodded. "Yeah, we got them. It's definitely our Brooke. Poor thing. No wonder she's so scared. That fuckwad dang near killed her!"

The sheriff shook his head. "No one should have to

go through that. Chicago police were worried when they couldn't contact her. They thought he might have already caught up with her."

"He won't if we have anything to do with it." Kent sounded angry as Brooke neared them, trembling.

"Amen to that!" The sheriff turned to go. "Well, I'll get Buchanan tucked in for the night and call his daddy. See you tomorrow. Good work, Deputy."

Brooke's blood ran cold. Deputy! Of all the nerve!

Chapter Ten

As soon as Mason Bains drove off, Kent turned to go back inside. He had been longing to get back to Brooke ever since he'd left her. He was surprised to see her behind him, and his heart fell into his boots when he saw the look of betrayal on her face.

"Brooke." He didn't know what else to say.

"Deputy?" She said it all.

Travis had waved to Jonah, who was getting into his car. He looked over at the standoff and sighed. He slowly ventured nearer.

"Can we talk?" Kent's voice was gentle, his face pensive.

Brooke shook her head sadly. "There's nothing to say."

"There's plenty to say." Kent's chin jutted out as determination overtook him.

"There's nothing to say that will make a difference."

Her voice was quiet. She turned around and went back inside.

Travis walked over to Kent, who stood watching her go. "Is that it?"

Kent looked up at him in despair. "She heard Mason call me deputy."

"And?"

"You saw her."

"Yes, I did. I also saw her pictures earlier, and I know we can't just let her go." Travis made it all sound so easy, but Kent knew he wasn't as laid-back about the situation as he was making out. They had both wept in each other's arms a few hours ago when Mason had sent through the pictures of a girl, beaten half to death, all alone, lying unconscious in a hospital bed. The report stated that she was in a coma; they didn't know whether she would survive. Her experience had been rather gruesome. The guys had vowed then and there that they would keep her safe.

"You're right. We can't let her go." Kent thought back to just a short while ago when he had held her, kissed her, loved her. He could never let her go again.

"Is there a back exit?" Travis stood next to Kent, watching the door.

"Not without setting off the fire alarm."

Travis grinned. He could just imagine Brooke's face if she did that. She would be so pissed! "So, we're just gonna wait?"

Kent's eyes narrowed. "Well we ain't making a scene in there."

Travis nodded, grinning. "I sure know what kind of scene I'd like to have with her, buddy." He sighed.

Kent grinned too. "Yeah, I saw her watching that threesome at Ty's. She's sure interested."

Travis chuckled. "There's a cure for that, you know?"

"Yeah, and I think we might just have the antidote she needs."

Brooke stormed back to the table where she had left her purse. She finished the wine left in her glass and then shuddered as she felt a familiar presence behind her, and smelled the distinctive scents of the two men she had just walked away from.

"Brooke, we need to talk." Kent used the same domineering voice he had used on Rich. Of course he would, he was the deputy, after all!

"Deputy, unless I am under arrest, I wish to leave, alone." Brooke turned to him, spitting the words out as Kent blocked her path.

She stared defiantly into his gorgeous green eyes that shone down at her.

"Of course you can leave. I'd just like to speak to outside before you go, that's all." Kent moved to one side, speaking calmly.

"Perhaps I didn't make myself clear. I said I wish to leave *alone*." Brooke spoke through gritted teeth.

"And perhaps I didn't make *myself* clear. I'd like to speak to you outside *Miss Anderson*." Kent hissed into her ear. Brooke turned hot with astonishment and anger. She stared at him. He cocked an expectant eyebrow at her and waited. Swallowing hard, Brooke slowly left the bar.

She waited in the deserted parking lot for the guys to follow her. She folded her arms and took deep breaths to steady her nerves.

"Baby, just give me a chance to explain," Kent pleaded with her, his voice softening.

"Explain what? That you're the deputy? Why would I care about that?" Brooke jutted out her chin defiantly.

"Because you *do* care, dammit. It bothers you. I get that. You're in trouble and you're worried I'm gonna do something to make it worse."

"So leave me alone and you can't make it worse," Brooke shouted, glad no one was about.

"Why won't you talk to me? You never tell me anything. I might just be able to help." Kent's voice was deep and loud, not quite a shout.

"Like you tell *me* everything, you mean, *deputy*?"

"I'm off duty for fuck's sake! I've been off all week. What difference does it make what job I do when I'm not even doing it?" Kent was shouting now and Travis moved closer.

"But you *have* been doing it!" she screamed at him, clenching her fists with frustration. "You haven't stopped interrogating me since I met you. You ruined everything with your constant questions. Well I hope you're happy with your answers now because I'm leaving!" Brooke barged past him angrily, but Travis caught up with her before she got very far.

"Darlin', I think it's about time we talked properly. Why don't you come up to the ranch with us tonight and we can have a civilized discussion about all this, huh?" Travis's voice was calm and laid-back, but the grip he had on her was anything but.

In her heart she knew he was making sense. She would love to go back to the ranch with them and make everything all right. But it was too late.

"Forget it! You should've told me he was the law. You practically lied to me. Just like everything else you said—it was all lies!" She choked the words out as the sobs welled in her throat.

"No, darlin'. No one lied. I didn't tell you about his job 'cause it didn't seem important, that's all." Travis loosened his grip and went to wrap an arm around her, but she flinched away.

"Don't you come near me, either of you. You've just been stringing me along to try and get information from me. I know you've been in touch with the cops in Chicago. That's how you got my name. And I know you've been talking about me behind my back. Well, it's none of your damn business, you hear? *I'm* none of your fucking business!"

"Miss Anderson, would you care to tell me why you

didn't turn up in court last week? The police verified that you signed the form confirming you would appear regarding the allegations you made about a Chad West, but then you didn't show up. They're concerned something might have happened to you. Did you not think to tell them you'd changed your mind?" Kent's voice was low and authoritative. He was definitely working now!

Brooke stared at him, aghast. "I don't know what you're talking about." Tears flooded her eyes and she trembled. She had been about to flounce off back to the hotel, but he had caught her totally off-guard.

"Did you know you were due to appear in court last week?" Kent asked slowly.

"No. I never signed anything. I couldn't, I wasn't there." Her mind raced.

"How long have you been running, darlin'?" Travis's voice was gentle.

Brooke sniffed and angrily wiped tears from her face. "Not long enough." She snapped the words out and took a step up the road.

"Brooke, baby, we only want to help you," Kent told her.

She swung back around to face him. Her face was scorching-hot with anger and tears. She took a deep breath, determined to get her words out without crying again.

"You can't help me, Kent. I went to the police. They said they would keep me safe. They lied. He caught up with me. They couldn't catch him and neither can you.

As far as I'm concerned, you're all just a bunch of liars, so I'm better off on my own. I don't need to listen to any more of your damn bullshit. I've heard enough. I'm leaving town first thing in the morning, so you won't have to waste any more time thinking up what shit you can feed me next. Now leave me alone!" She stormed up the road, letting the tears flood her face. All she wanted to do was lie down and cry.

It was dark and the street was deserted. Travis watched her go. Even though she didn't want their help, he was darned if he wasn't going to make sure she got back to the hotel safely. He and Kent followed her from a safe distance and didn't speak until they saw her enter the front door of the Montgomery.

"We've lost her, bro." Kent had tears in his eyes as they turned back to fetch the pickup.

Travis said nothing. His mind was in a whirl.

"I blew it, didn't I?" Kent said as he stared out the window of the truck.

"No. She just doesn't trust the law, that's all. You're the deputy around here. She would have found out soon enough." Travis sighed and took a hand off the wheel to run through his hair. He remembered the feel of Brooke stroking his hair earlier, and his gut wrenched.

"I held her tonight. I held her and I kissed her and I touched her and...I loved her, dammit. *I love her*, Travis."

Kent stared at his lover as the realization evidently hit him.

Travis put his hand on Kent's. "I know, buddy. I love her too. We've just got to figure out a way of convincing *her* that." He smiled as Kent lifted his hand and kissed the back of it.

The rest of their journey was spent deep in thought. They arrived at the ranch and headed straight for the bedroom.

Travis was the first to undress and head to the en suite to brush his teeth. "We need to be at the hotel early, before she gets chance to leave," he announced as he went back through to the bedroom. His mouth turned up into a wicked grin at the sight of Kent, naked, staring out the window. The moonlight cast a soft glow over his ripped body, accentuating his muscular frame. Kent turned around slowly to face him, as Travis handed him his toothbrush, fully loaded with paste.

Travis cleared his throat and continued with his plan. "We'll block off her exit with the pickup and refuse to move it until she changes her mind."

Kent burst out laughing and went to rinse his mouth. "She'll kill us, bro, you know that, don't you?" he called from the en-suite.

"What a way to go!" Travis sniggered as he climbed into bed.

Kent grinned as he climbed in next to him. "Well now, seeing as we both might be six feet under tomorrow,

I think we'd best make the most of the time we have left, don't you?"

Travis chortled as he took his lover in his arms. "I like the way you think, buddy."

Brooke was grateful that no one was about when she let herself into the Montgomery Hotel and crept upstairs. She couldn't face anyone right now. Tears blurred her vision, and her legs felt like lead. She locked herself in her bedroom before throwing herself onto the bed. She lay there, sobbing into her pillow.

Everything was wrong. Her whole life was shit. She was still on the run after nearly six months and couldn't see a way of stopping. If Chad ever caught up with her, she knew he would kill her.

If only her parents hadn't died. If only she had some family she could turn to. But she didn't. She was alone. No matter how much she longed to have someone to lean on, she knew it wasn't going to happen.

As she drifted into an exhausted sleep, her mind meandered to thoughts of the two guys who had held her earlier that evening. Could a ménage work? She knew they were both dominant and would want to look after her. Both guys had an air of authority about them and a presence that made her feel safe and cared for. Would they both want her at the same time? Would she really be able to lie in the arms of them both together? She thought of Kent's wonderful, soft body and how lovely it would be to snuggle up to him in bed. With his deep voice, he would tell her what he wanted her to do. *Strip for me, play with yourself, kiss me.*

Travis would lean into her from the other side, his musky scent and low drawl urging her on, encouraging her. *Let me see your gorgeous pussy, darlin', spread those luscious legs wide for me. It's OK, you can do it.*

Brooke would strip off for them while they lay on the bed watching her. They would be wearing nothing but their jeans. She would see their erections strain beneath the denim, and watch their eyes glaze over with lust as they gazed at her. She would feel the cool air as she removed her shirt, and her nipples would tighten in her lace bra. She would bend down, giving them a front-row view of her ass as she peeled off her jeans. She could hear them gasping as she slowly unfastened her bra, and then her large breasts would bounce free as she threw the clothing onto the floor. Slowly, very slowly, she would tuck her thumbs into the waist of her panties before gradually sliding them down over her hips, her thighs, and ultimately discarding them.

She could see her two men with their arms outstretched, bidding her to join them on the bed, and she would waste no time in crawling up the bed to reach them. Kent would tenderly kiss her mouth while Travis's hot tongue would caress the back of her neck, finding that secret little place that made her shudder. Their masculine scents would envelope her in a cloud of love and safety. Travis's calloused hands would graze down her back, causing her to shiver deliciously, while Kent would fondle her soft breasts while his tongue tangled with hers.

Her breathing hitched as they both ran their hands up and down her sensitized body, kissing and licking her as they went. She watched her own nipples grow darker, turning into large, hard nubs. Both men murmured sweet words and encouragement to her, making her feel beautiful and confident.

When they ran their fingers over her pulsating pussy, they would find it dripping wet, eagerly awaiting their pleasure. Their fingers probed inside her saturated channel to find her G-spot, that elusive place Chad didn't even bother to look for. She would buck under their ministrations, and Travis would finger-fuck her while kissing and sucking at her clit. Kent would lavish her with soft kisses, murmuring to her all the time, keeping her on the edge by tweaking her nipples relentlessly.

Travis would say those magical words she had read in books, but never heard. *Come for me, darlin'*, and she would let go—*really* let go—and scream her orgasm while clutching her men and holding on for dear life. Brooke just knew that these men would be capable of wringing the most excruciating orgasms from her body. They would make them last and not be satisfied until they knew she couldn't possibly take any more, and then they would hold her *and love her*. They would help her, encourage her, reassure her that she was doing well. They would buoy her confidence. They would allow her to make as much noise as she wanted, and to touch them wherever and whenever she wanted.

When she was ready, they would both make love to her. Kent would be slow and gentle. His cock would be thick and sturdy. It would stretch her wide open and pound into her, caressing her G-spot, a place she had almost convinced herself she didn't have. He would kiss her as she came, and she would scream deliriously into his mouth. Her body would be racked with aftershocks, and he would hold her gently as she floated on a cloud of ecstasy. He would nuzzle her ear and smother her breasts in warm kisses. His hot seed would shoot into her womb and she would hear him groan as he came. His soft arms would envelope her and hold her while they both calmed their breathing and returned slowly back to earth.

Travis would be a passionate lover. He would run his calloused hands over her body, causing her nipples to stand to attention and sensitizing her skin. He would read every expression and sound she made and gauge his actions accordingly. His cock would be thick and long. He would ensure she was well ready for him before thrusting his throbbing member into her dripping pussy, reaching every nerve ending she had. He would thrust passionately, causing her to groan and gasp with every movement. She would be riding a wave of euphoria as he took her higher and higher before commanding her to come for him. She would scream loud and long as she tipped over the edge and bright colors and sparkling lights danced in front of her eyes. He would give a huge grunt as he forced his boiling seed into her waiting womb, over and over again. She would cling to his frame as their bodies shook, her nails digging cruelly into his hard flesh. He would groan with delight and hold her as though he would never let go, and they would lay panting, sweating, and loving each other.

And they really would *love* her. She would know it. Feel it. Their love would surround her like a cloak, protecting her from the world. And she would love them back. Lordy, how she would love them! She would do anything for them. She would cook for them while they were working. She would keep their lovely home clean and tidy for them. She would love taking care of their laundry. When they weren't working, they could all go riding together. They could go for picnics and long walks. They would all be so happy together. They would always be laughing and joking. Life would be perfect.

If only...

$$\textit{Chapter Eleven}$$

Travis woke shortly before five o'clock the next morning. He didn't quite know what had disturbed him but he knew something was off. He opened the window and the stench of smoke hit him straightaway, accompanied by the panicked whinnying of the horses. Black smoke billowed against the orange dawn, and red flames licked the tiled roof of the stable block.

"Kent, stable fire!" He pulled on his jeans and boots and fled down the hall while Kent made himself half-decent.

Hal's dusty pickup drew up onsite just as Travis was opening all the doors to allow the horses to run free. The heat was phenomenal as soon as he opened each stall. The fire had already taken hold, and the terrified horses were bucking manically trying to escape. Their hooves thundered over the yard, and they just kept running.

Kent ran up behind Hal with the hosepipe and got to work on the remains of the building.

"Mustard's still in there, I'm going to get him," Travis yelled, pointing to the back of one of the stalls. Kent nodded and pointed the hose in that direction as Travis crouched low and made his way toward his favorite horse. Mustard was huddled against the back wall of his stall, trembling with fear. All around them, the fire cracked and the clanking of falling debris made them both jump.

"Steady, boy," Travis cajoled him as he ventured nearer. The intense heat made his eyes stream, and he wiped sweat from his forehead. Mustard suddenly bucked, and Travis leapt back, slamming his back hard onto the stone floor. He was momentarily winded but managed to crawl to his feet, still soothing the massive horse, and patted its flank.

"The roof!" Hal shrieked as part of the stable roof caved in behind Travis.

"Fuck!" Kent hollered as he pointed the hose onto the burning rubble. "Travis, move!"

Travis led Mustard out of the remains of his stall as quickly as he could, narrowly missing some burning slats from the rapidly collapsing roof. He was choking badly but put a hand up to signal to Kent that he was OK.

After ensuring the horse was safe, and taking some deep breaths, Travis ran back to his partner. Hal had already liberated the surviving horses.

"Help's on its way," Kent promised. Travis and Hal

threw buckets of water on the burning debris while Kent continued with the hose.

"How many did we lose?" Travis called over to Hal.

"Four, all from the bottom end," Hal shouted.

Travis ran a hand through his hair before going back to refill his bucket. Not only did he love his livestock, but four horses was a lot of bucks! The boys weren't short on money, but losing four fine horses would certainly sting.

Gradually, more and more of their mountain neighbors came to help out with fighting the fire, and it was under control by the time the county firefighters arrived to finish the job.

"Hope you've got some coffee on?" Mason Bains teased as they pulled back to let the experts take over.

Kent grinned, leading him toward the house. A large man with gray hair and a stern expression approached them as they reached the door.

"Sheriff, I'll take the boy back with me if that's all right with you?" he asked in a deep, gruff voice.

"No problem, Frank. He's all yours." Mason grinned as the man nodded and went to find his wayward son.

"You let Rich out, then?" Kent said with a chuckle.

"I had no choice. When I got your call, I figured you'd need all the help you could get. I told him to consider it community service." Mason laughed.

"Well we're much obliged to you for that," Kent said with a weary chuckle.

Travis had seen off most of their friends and neighbors, who were now headed back down the mountain.

He sighed as he faced the smoldering wreck the fire-fighters were still damping down. He could see Hal over in the paddock where he had managed to round up most of the horses.

"Message for you from Hal, sir." One of the stable hands approached Travis as he stood surveying the damage. "Frank Buchanan's already sent some of his wranglers out to round up the last of the horses. Hal said not to worry; he'll meet you inside shortly."

"Thank you." Travis smiled and turned back toward the house as the young man hurried back to his duties.

"Here you go." Mason handed Travis a mug of strong coffee as soon as he entered the house. "Kent's gone for a shower; he'll be back in a minute."

Travis nodded. "Thanks."

"The fire chief'll be back soon too. He thinks he might have found something but he wants to check it out," Mason went on.

"Are we talking arson?" Kent's large frame filled the kitchen doorway. He was dressed in Levis and a smart red shirt, his fair hair still wet from his shower.

"It looks possible. We'll know more when he gets back," Mason said with a grave look on his face.

"I'll get cleaned up, let me know when he gets here." Travis took his coffee with him and headed for the bathroom.

The hot water soothed his aching muscles and washed the grime from his battered body. Once dried and dressed, he returned to the kitchen to find that the fire chief had just arrived.

"I'm afraid it's not good news," the chief told them with a frown.

Kent handed him some coffee.

"Looks to me like they'll have to replace that stable block completely," Mason Bains remarked as he and the chief sat at the little table in the kitchen.

"I suppose they can thank their lucky stars it didn't manage to spread to the house." The chief sighed.

"*Someone* can thank their lucky stars! If I get hold of them, they're dead meat." Travis was now dressed in a gray plaid shirt and clean jeans. He had thrown his other ones in the trash; there was no way he'd ever get the stench of smoke out of them. The heels of his boots clipped across the floor as he went over to join them at the table.

"Now don't you go taking the law into your own hands, Travis. Kent, you might need to keep a close eye on him," Mason admonished.

Kent sat down next to Travis and they resumed their coffees. "Well now, Sheriff, I might have to warn you that there's a distinct possibility I'll be helping him. You might want to look the other way while we kill the fuck-er." Kent had a face like thunder.

Mason sighed.

"Well, gentlemen, I have to inform you that this was most definitely an arson attack," the chief began. "We detected gasoline in the wreckage at the far end of the stables and some had soaked into the floor of the stalls."

"Fuck!" Travis's fist hit the table, making them all jump.

Kent's lips had tightened to a thin, straight line, and he closed his eyes momentarily as the news sank in.

"Do you guys have any enemies I need to know about?" Mason Bains studied the faces of the two cowboys in front of him.

"None that we know of," Kent replied.

"Have you had to arrest anyone lately that might bear a grudge?" The sheriff was clearly racking his own brain for the answers too. He and Kent worked closely together. There was no way either could be involved in any kind of incident without the other knowing about it. Besides, they spent half their time filing reports. Everything that happened in Moone was documented.

"Only Rich Buchanan a few times lately, but he was in the cell at the time. Besides, he would never do anything to harm a horse, even one of ours," Kent said with a pout.

A murderous expression crossed Travis's face and he leapt to his feet. "It's a fucking diversion! We need to get to Brooke!"

He ran to the door and threw himself into the pickup with a bemused Kent following him. Mason climbed into his SUV and followed them as they high-tailed it down the mountain.

"Where is she?" Travis demanded as he burst into the

foyer of the Montgomery. He had noticed that her beat-up car wasn't in the parking lot and feared the worst. Stella was just coming out of the restaurant.

"If you're looking for Brooke, she left about an hour ago. She tried to call you but…"

"Where did she go? Which direction?" Kent must have quickly cottoned on to Travis's conclusion, as his cop brain seemed to be working overtime.

"She didn't say exactly. She was going home, though, I think—Chicago," Stella sputtered. "Yes, that's right. She's got to get back to work."

Travis snorted, knowing full well she didn't have a job to get back to, let alone a home, by all accounts.

"You said she tried to call?" Kent was clearly trying hard to stay calm.

"Yes, she said she might have got it all wrong last night. She said she'd been upset but that now she's had time to think things through. She wanted to talk to you but didn't know if she'd be welcome at the ranch, so she wanted to ring first. She tried several times but no one answered. She assumed you didn't want to speak to her, so she left. I could tell she was upset," Stella explained sadly.

"Fuck!" Everything was adding up in Travis's mind, and he clenched his fists angrily. "We need to get after her!"

"I'll follow you." Mason was right behind the boys as they rushed out the door. "Stella, you get Jolene to radio through to me if you hear anything, OK?" he shouted over to her.

"That's where her car was parked, isn't it?" Kent stopped suddenly, staring at the ground. He bent down and put his hand on some drops of liquid lying on the yard where her car had been.

"Whatcha got there?" Mason had stopped to pick up a piece of litter, which he started to unfurl as he hurried over to Kent.

"Some kind of oil or something, I think, but I'm not sure." Kent was sniffing it.

Travis huffed and went over to see what was delaying them. He stared at Kent's hand where he'd smeared the liquid. He bent over and smelled it. "Brake fluid!" he shouted, his face turning white.

"Wait. I found this. It was over there." Mason held up a crumpled piece of paper with one word printed on it. "GOTCHA!"

Brooke had woken just after six a.m. She felt stiff and uncomfortable but was in a good mood. She had lay there thinking about the wonderful dream she had just had. She couldn't help smiling when she thought about making love with her two cowboys. Her cowboys?

She had to admit that she had no right thinking of them as hers, although she remembered they had already referred to her as theirs, so maybe there was some hope after all. She had been thinking about how wonderful it would be if she could stay on Moone Mountain with them. She loved it here and had made some wonderful friends whom she would miss like mad if she left. The laid-back lifestyle was so much easier to cope with than the hustle and bustle of Chicago, and she would love to live in the ranch house halfway up the mountain instead of in some pokey little apartment.

She had even started to think that maybe Kent would be able to help her. He had already found out about her without her telling him anything, so he was obviously good at his job. Perhaps he would be the one to find Chad and lock him up. It was a lovely thought and one that had sent her drifting back into another blissful dream.

It hadn't taken her long to shower and dress, and most of her belongings were already in her bag as she still hadn't unpacked properly. She had found Stella downstairs and told her over breakfast about her thoughts. She had been delighted that Stella had approved of her idea of staying and trying to make a go of things with Travis and Kent.

She really didn't dare just turn up at the ranch after her reaction to the guys last night and was thrilled when Stella handed her a phone and the number to call. There had been no answer at first, and she assumed Travis must already be working on the ranch. After last night, she hadn't expected him to be up this early. Kent must have been having a lie-in, or helping out.

She had spent the next hour becoming more and more despondent as her calls continued to go unanswered. Slowly it had dawned on her that they probably guessed it was she who was calling and didn't want to speak to her. Served her right for walking out on them last night!

Loneliness had suddenly washed over her, and she realized she had no reason to stay in Moone. She had said a tearful good-bye to Stella and thrown her bags in the car. A piece of paper on the windshield caught her eye, and her blood froze as she read the word printed on it. "GOTCHA!"

Chad was here! She crumpled it up angrily and threw it on the ground before clambering into the driver's seat. Her brakes squealed as she sped out of the parking lot, and she drove hell-bent for leather out of town.

Not knowing where she was going, she just kept on driving. Her heart was hammering and she heaved in gulps of air to keep from panting. Her mind was spinning out of control, and she had to speak aloud to try to calm herself. She tried to focus on the road and her driving to try to stop her whirling thoughts. There was only one thought she should be worrying about and that was to just keep driving. Chad had been in Moone. He might still be there. She checked her rearview mirror constantly but was confident she wasn't being followed.

After a few miles, a road sign indicated another town coming up. On one hand, it might be safer with people around if anything happened, but then people might notice her, and if Chad went that way and asked around, they would confirm which way she had gone. On reflection, she decided it was safer to take the alternative route that led through the countryside. With any luck no one would see her there, not even Chad.

The country roads were winding and narrow, and she began to wonder if this had been the best way to go after all. She had to slow down as she approached yet another blind bend, and her heart leapt. She was sure she had seen a car behind her. As soon as it was safe to do so, she sped up, but the car continued to follow, gaining on her. A cold chill ran up her spine when she caught a good glimpse of the car—a pale blue sports car. In that second she would have given anything for it to have been a few shades darker and a good few years younger—making it Rich Buchanan's—but it wasn't. It was definitely Chad's.

She pushed her foot to the floor and yanked the stick shift into gear before accelerating as hard as she could. It was no good. Her car was no match for his. She broke again for another sharp bend and was horrified to find that the car didn't slow. It hardly reacted at all. She took the bend at a dangerous speed, praying that nothing was coming the other way. It wasn't. But as soon as the road straightened out again, she felt a massive jolt as the car behind nudged her trunk. She shrieked and stared into the rearview mirror. Chad's face was contorted into an ugly sneer as he watched her cringe. She snapped her head around to the front again and hit the gas hard. He was on her tail the whole time. Another bend was coming up with a car heading toward her.

Brooke hit the brake and nothing happened. She pumped the pedal frantically, but she continued to whizz headlong toward the bend—and the oncoming car. She veered to the side of the road, praying they could pass safely, even at that speed, but her prayer went unanswered. She hauled the steering wheel out of the path of the other car, and her vehicle swerved off the road and into woodland. For a fraction of a section, she thought she might be OK, that the rough terrain might just slow the car down enough for it to stop. Then she saw the line of trees blocking her route. She continued to pump the brake, but it was no good. She yanked on the steering wheel and the car slid sideways into the thick, calloused bark of one of the trees. Searing pain coursed through her body just before the whole world went dark.

Travis's foot was constantly to the floor of his pickup as he sped along the familiar roads outside town. He could see Mason in his rearview mirror. Mason was a good man, and Travis trusted him to help all he could. He just hoped that they weren't too late.

"I can't believe I let her down again." Kent cursed as he stared out of the windshield.

"Like you had a choice, buddy? That fuckwad knew exactly how to stop us from saving our girl. Anything else and we would've left it and run down to that hotel. He would have guessed that we couldn't just leave the horses to burn to death!"

"So what if *she* burns to death? There were two pools of fluid, bro—those brakes of hers have been cut front and back. She doesn't stand a chance!" Kent's voice was low and his face was white.

"Let's just concentrate on finding her, shall we? Town or country?"

Kent looked up in surprise at the question, and then seemed to realize where they were. "There's pros and cons to both of them, but my guess is she'll go for country. She'll feel safer if there's no one around." He sighed. Travis didn't blame him. Everything was riding on Kent's deduction skills.

"I agree. We go this way." Travis steered the car toward the country road and then cursed when he had to slow down. "Fuck! Those dang brakes won't last long on these roads."

Kent closed his eyes momentarily, and Travis realized he should have kept his mouth shut. Poor Kent blamed himself for everything. He was sure to blame himself for this too, even though Lord knows he couldn't have done anything to prevent it.

"Come on, bud, you need to be looking out for that beat-up old banger of hers. With any luck, she'll have holed up somewhere to check her map or something." He knew it was a long shot, but he had to keep positive for Kent's sake. Once the deputy got into one of his funks, it could be days before he climbed back out, and Travis needed him more than ever right now.

Both guys pricked up their ears when they heard Jolene's cheery voice come over the radio.

"Hi, Sheriff, Deputy. I just got a call from Stella at the Montgomery, said I need to call you right away. She was cleaning out Brooke Adams's room and she found something under the bed. She said she thought it looked like a letter, a sort of statement. Anyway, it claims that she lied to the police about some guy beating her up and says she just tried to get him into trouble 'cause he dumped her. There's a long list of stuff she's accused him of and the letter says it's all bullshit, or words to that effect. Says she sustained all her scars before she even met Chad West, and that she doesn't know who attacked her in the alley that night. Does that mean something to you?"

Mason Bains let out a big sigh over the radio. "Yes. Thanks, Jolene. Let me know if you hear anything else."

"Will do, Sheriff."

"Bullshit! She didn't cut her own brakes, did she? And who wrote the note?" Travis snorted.

"Well it's possible those things were planted to hold up her story if she *is* trying to implicate this guy in something," Mason replied.

"I saw those welts on her body, Sheriff, and some of them were definitely recent. She was with that fucker for at least a year that we know of. He did it, I'm telling you." Travis was certain.

"What do you reckon, Deputy?"

Kent thought for a minute. "The only thing she ever told us was her name, and that wasn't entirely true." Kent pouted as he spoke. He seemed to go real cold. Poor Kent probably didn't want to think of her as a liar.

"Yeah, but it didn't hurt anyone. The only thing it did was stop you from helping her. That's not a crime, is it?" Travis was adamant.

"No. It wasn't really a lie, either. Her first name is definitely Brooke and, to be honest, her surname is really none of our business. That girl's not a liar, boss. I believe in her. Did she definitely write that letter they found?" Kent frowned. None of this was adding up.

"No, I think Jolene said it was typed but not signed. Why would she be carrying it around with her, though, if she wasn't trying to use it as evidence?" Mason replied thoughtfully.

"Well that's it, then. She hasn't signed it. She probably never even wrote it, or if she did, it was under duress. I believe in her, boss. She's the kindest, sweetest, most adorable thing I ever... Shit!" Kent stared in disbelief at the sight of the twisted-up wreck nestled in the trees to the side of the road.

Travis could hear his heart thudding from the other side of the truck. Travis said nothing. He veered off the road and pulled up in front of the crashed car. His heart was in his boots as he followed Kent over to the mashed metal.

"Brooke? Baby, are you there?" Kent's voice sounded

strangled as he called out. The passenger door had hit the tree first, but the metal had concertinaed. If Brooke was in there, it was doubtful she'd be in any state to call back to him.

Travis tried to get his arm in through a broken window to try to feel for her. There was no way either of them could get inside; it was too wrecked. Kent was searching the area, presumably hoping for signs of her or her belongings. Travis knew that he would be hoping—as he was—that Brooke had got out before the car smashed into the trees.

"I'd lay a dollar to a penny she's gone," Mason said gravely as he walked over to them.

Travis shook his head. "I can't find anything in there," he confirmed.

"Look." Mason pointed to some tire tracks that had come off the road and stopped in front of the trees. It appeared that the same tracks then wound in a loop back onto the road.

"The fuckwad's got her!" Travis's eyes were staring in disbelief.

"Come on, bro." Kent was already running toward the pickup. Seconds later, the two cars rejoined the road while three hearts pounded like thunder.

Chapter Twelve

"There's no way she got out of that wreck by herself. She either got out before the crash or *he* got her out after." Kent was staring out the window, trying to make sense of it all.

"Unless she got out and ran?" Travis kept his eyes peeled for any sign of her as he drove carefully through the winding country lanes.

Kent shook his head. "Even if she got out before the car hit that tree, she was going way too fast to walk away from it."

"So the fuckwad either got her out or caught up with her as she tried to escape. Where the hell would he take her to? There's no buildings or anything around here, is there?" Travis frowned.

Kent shook his head. "Possibly the odd wood shack, but that's all. No one lives out here that I know of."

Travis sighed.

They traveled on for what seemed forever. It was difficult to decide whether to go slow enough to look out for any sign of them or to speed up in case he had high-tailed it out of there once he'd gotten her.

"I think we need to split up, boys," Mason called over the radio. "You keep checking the area while I step on it in case he's making a run for it."

"I agree," Kent replied. "Keep in touch."

With that, the sheriff's SUV overtook them and sped off into the distance. Travis huffed. He probably wanted to be the one putting his foot down and getting on with the job instead of slowly driving down the lanes looking out for signs of life. He'd understand that Mason could drive a lot faster than he could, though, so he'd let it go.

The air was getting cooler, and Kent felt the cold deep in his bones. He couldn't tell Travis that the likelihood of her still being alive was dwindling by the minute. From what he had read about Chad West, he was a desperate man. Not only were the cops in Chicago after him, but they had put out calls for his arrest everywhere from there to Colorado and beyond. No one was going to pass up the opportunity to get scum like that off the streets; attacking a woman was one crime that even the most lenient cops wouldn't tolerate. Kent prided himself on being the fairest lawman he could be, but he was also a lover and would do everything in his power to save that girl.

"You don't believe all that shit about her lying about

the accusations, do you?" Travis's question yanked him from his thoughts.

"No, I don't." He spoke without even thinking.

Travis grinned, nodding slowly.

"I know what you're thinking," Kent said without even looking at him. "I wasn't sure if we could trust her at first. When I found out she lied about her name, I figured she probably lied about other stuff too. I was wrong. I admit it. I just had to know. I needed to be certain she was for real. She seemed too perfect; I was suspicious. We both sensed she was in some kind of trouble, and with the scars and everything, it just went right on to prove it. I just wanted to know which side of the law she was in trouble with, that's all."

"Did it matter?" Travis studied him thoughtfully.

Kent shook his head. "Nope. I just figured it was easier knowing what we were dealing with, you know?" He shrugged, looking over at his partner.

Travis grinned. "Yeah, I know, buddy. If she'd told us what the hell was going on, we wouldn't be here now. But she had her reasons. She had to know if she could trust us."

"You think she knows yet?"

"I think the fact that she spent all that time trying to call us this morning would suggest that she does," Travis drawled.

"I think so too," Kent added decisively.

Travis sighed. "So we better not let her down."

Kent frowned and picked up the radio. "Any news yet, boss?"

Mason Bains sounded cross. "No sign. I don't reckon he could've got this far without me seeing him. It's one straight road up here; there's nowhere to hide. I'm coming back your way. Chances are he's slipped onto a country lane somewhere, skulking around like the coward he is."

"OK, boss." Kent frowned. "He's got to be around here somewhere, bro. He'll likely know we're coming after him and try to bide his time until we give up." He peered out of the window intently again.

"He don't know us, does he?" Travis shook his head incredulously.

"Nope. If he thinks we're gonna give up on our girl, he's got another think coming."

Travis grinned at his lover's determination.

They traveled on in silence for a while, both staring out the windows. Most of the roads were nothing but dirt tracks, and the men shook about as the truck bounced up and down over the rocks and mud.

"There!" Travis suddenly shouted, gaping at the empty road ahead.

Kent focused on the spot he was looking at. "We've got him!" He spoke through gritted teeth.

"Come in, Sheriff," Kent spoke into the radio as Travis neared the track lines that had kicked a heap of mud off the road and onto the grass verge. They were headed into a forest.

"Go ahead."

"Sheriff, we've got something. Tire tracks leading off into the forest." Kent was calm but his heart was thumping in anticipation.

Travis followed the muddy tracks through lush grass, maneuvering carefully between the trees. Kent relayed their location as best he could, clinging to the grip bar above his door as the truck ricocheted over the rough terrain. Four eyes and four ears searched in every direction for some sign of life. The track seemed to go on forever.

"Through there!" Kent pointed to what looked like part of a wooden structure partially hidden among the trees.

Travis drove as close as he could, seeing that it was a derelict old barn or shack one of the local farmers must have used at one time. Trees blocked their route, given the width of the pickup, so they would have to walk the rest of the way. Kent informed Mason of their approximate position before following his partner out of the vehicle. They cautiously made their way through the trees, checking their surroundings as they went.

"*Car.*" Travis mouthed the word as he pointed to a piece of blue metal half-secluded around the side of the shack. Kent nodded. Stealthily they crept though the long grass and neared the disused shack.

Suddenly a scream froze them both to the spot. It wasn't an ear-piercing, loud shriek; this was a weak cry of desperation. The men stared at each other before bursting into action. They ran over to the shack, slowing their steps as they neared it. They peered through a broken window at a sight that numbed their very souls.

Brooke's eyes felt heavy as she slowly opened them to find herself lying on a hard wooden bench in what looked like a tumbled-down shed. Every part of her body hurt, her back burning with the sting of a whip and she groaned in pain.

"Shut up, slut." She recognized the callous voice that snarled at her, and every hair on her body stood up on end. A frozen chill seared through her whole being and for a fraction of a second she wished she was already dead.

"Sit up, you fat, lazy cow." Chad came into her blurred line of sight, and she moaned uncontrollably as he kicked the bench she was lying on. More pain coursed through her from her head to her feet.

"Ch-Chad?"

"Who else?" he sneered. "I told you to sit up!"

His voice resounded in her throbbing head, and she tried to pull herself up. Too late. He kicked the bench again, and the pain was unbearable as the vibration ricocheted down her back. She shrieked in agony and then cowered as his massive frame towered angrily over her. Placing her bloody hands on either side of the bench, she forced herself to sit up. The pain scorched through her back, and she bit her lip hard to keep from screaming. Her head was swimming as she rose, and the room seemed to spin around her in dingy hues of brown. Light streamed in through broken windows and half the roof that was missing. It burned her eyes, and she squeezed them shut in defense. The stench of damp wood and sweat assaulted her.

"Hurry up!" Chad's clipped, threatening voice planted more dread inside her, and she felt as though she was about to vomit as she slowly turned herself around to look at him.

"At fucking long last. Are you gonna take this long to do everything you're told to?" he shouted through gritted teeth, and she winced.

"N-no," she replied weakly, still trying to focus her eyes. She swayed slightly as she tried to balance, and gripped the top of the bench as blood ran off her hands onto the wooden floor.

"No what? Haven't you learned anything, slut?"

"Yes...I mean...no...no, sir," she stammered. Her brain felt like marshmallow and she couldn't think straight. It seemed to irritate him even more.

"Halle-fucking-lujah!" he sneered.

She was staring up at him, trying to focus on his face. It was still blurry, but the more she peered at it, the more it seemed to clarify. His eyes were small and gray. They looked cold and mean. He had a long nose that she remembered thinking looked manly, almost Roman; now she saw that it was skinny and little out of line with the rest of his face. His lips were thin and formed a small slit across his pale skin. His dirty-blond hair was straggly and just hung in straight lines down to his shoulders. This wasn't the man she remembered at all! She had thought he was a very handsome man, with an authoritative demeanor that commanded respect from everyone around him. As time had gone on, she had thought he was frightening, brutal, but still attractive. Now she saw before her an ugly, puny coward. How had she not seen that before? His face seemed to be contorted into a permanent sneer, making him look even more grotesque.

"Like what you see?" He raised both his eyebrows, which gave him a very odd expression. She suddenly envisaged Travis raising one sexy eyebrow as he gazed at her, and a fire began to burn in her stomach. She closed her eyes for a second to enjoy the sensation and then snapped them open when she heard Chad.

"Trying to take it all in, are you? See what you've been missing?"

He grabbed her arms and she whimpered at the pain. One arm felt heavy and limp, and she wondered if it might be broken. The pain that penetrated it was almost unbearable. Chad obviously sensed this as he squeezed that arm even tighter. *Bastard!* She did her best not to make a sound as she knew he would hurt her even more. This was a game he liked to play. A game that had almost killed her on a couple of occasions.

She looked down at his arm. He was strong but scrawny. His fingers were long and skinny, with bones protruding all over the place. Even his nails were disgusting—dirty and well-chewed. She had never noticed that about him before.

"Talk to me, bitch!" He squeezed her arms even tighter and shook her. Pain racked her whole body, and she had to bite her tongue to keep from yelling out.

"W-what do you want?" Her voice shook with agony and fear.

"Apart from the obvious, you mean, slut?" He licked his lips, and she felt his eyes burn into her skin. Her stomach churned. She just stared at him in horror. He couldn't be serious, surely?

"You and me have some unfinished business to take care of first, though, don't we? Or should that be *during*?" He gave a disgusting laugh, which sent a cold shiver right through her painful body.

Oh God no!

Something cool ran down her head and into her eye, making her vision blurry again. Brooke lifted her good arm, and he actually let it go while she wiped her eye with the back of her hand. To her horror, she saw it was blood. She must have cut her head. Suddenly a vision of the tree came into her mind and she recalled the accident. She had swerved to avoid driving headlong into a row of trees and ended up colliding side-on instead. She recalled yanking the steering wheel around so the empty passenger side would hit first and had tried to angle it so the back of the car would be worst hit. It didn't seem to have made any difference as she felt like shit. She must have hit it hard to be in this much agony.

She slowly tried to feel each of her limbs and body parts in turn. Her arm must be broken; it lay there, limp and lifeless, throbbing like heck. She felt something wrong with her back, but she had managed to sit up so it couldn't be too bad. Her legs felt weird. They were heavy and felt like Jell-O. Pain was searing through them both, but she knew they couldn't be broken or she wouldn't have been able to move them, let alone bend them at the knees. Her head throbbed, and she now knew she had done some damage to it. Her abdomen was just a mass of pain. There was nothing she could pinpoint there; it just hurt like the devil.

She suddenly became aware that he had been talking to her. His voice sounded mushy and far away. She tried to look up at him, but her eyes were trying to close.

"Don't you dare pass out on me!" His harsh voice cut into her, and she flicked her eyes straight up at him. She had heard him say this before on many occasions and knew what the consequences would be if she fainted. She forced herself to stay focused as the mush slowly dissipated. The pain shot through her as he squeezed and shook her back to the present.

Brooke realized she had little hope of escaping with all her injuries. At the same time, though, she was determined not to let him win this time. He had taken enough of her past. If she could just get through the present, she might still have hope for the future. Her mind whirled.

There had to be a way out of this somehow. For now, though, she would just go along with what he wanted, and do her best to stall him as long as she could. At best she would give herself time to be rescued. At worst...

She grappled with her thoughts to try to concentrate on their conversation. "Unfinished business?" She decided it safer to contemplate that aspect of his ramblings, rather than the rest, which didn't bear thinking about.

Apparently satisfied that she was still with him, he smirked. "Yes, I believe you had a visitor right before you ran off like a scalded cat."

She stared at him in disbelief. Scalded cat? She suddenly felt angry as well as indignant. How dare he imply that she had done something wrong? Brooke controlled her breathing and kept her face as expressionless as she could. Although she was seething inside, she knew better than to let him know she was annoyed. She had been punished too many times to remember just for a look he accused her of having.

"H-he said you sent him. I didn't know if it was true." She spoke in a quiet voice.

"You knew full well it was true! You've seen Kenny loads of times. Why else would he be there? He gave you something to sign, didn't he?"

"Y-yes...but..."

"But you didn't sign it." He said the words slowly and carefully as if speaking to child who wouldn't understand him.

Brooke would have felt better if he had shouted at her. This patronizing crap always meant he was leading up to something—something real bad. She stared at him, wide-eyed. Fear and anger mixed within her, and she did her best to quell them both.

"Why didn't you sign it, Brooke?" That voice again. *Shit!*

She didn't know what to tell him. She just shrugged sadly.

"Well now. If you can't answer that question, how's about another one? Why did you tell the cops I raped you and beat you up?" His voice was threateningly calm.

Brooke shook uncontrollably. She stared into his cruel little eyes. Anger and fear were still battling it out inside her, and just when she thought fear was in the lead anger romped home.

"Because you did." The words spat out of her mouth, astounding her as much as him.

His patronizing expression was replaced with red-faced rage, and she braced herself for the onslaught.

"How dare you! After everything I've done for you! How could you make up such filthy lies about me?" His voice resounded around the room, and his face was right up close to hers. She could smell his rancid breath as he yelled at her.

Pain coursed through her body as he tightened his grip on her, and anger rose up to meet it. Her thoughts were racing. She took a deep breath, letting anger take pole position once again. It was way better than the alternative, and if he was going to kill her anyway, she'd rather tell him what she thought of him first.

"You raped me! You beat me up and left me for dead, just like you're about to do now, no doubt. You ruined my life! You wrecked my body. I know you're going to kill me today, and I know you'll torture me in the process. Well guess what? I don't give a damn. And you wanna know why? Because I'm finished. I would rather be dead than live the rest of my life fearing you, running away all the time just in case you catch up with me! I can't have a life this way. I refuse to. So go ahead, fuckwad—kill me!" Her heart pumped indignant anger through her body in massive bursts, and she just couldn't stop herself. She knew she was going to pay for it, but so what? She stared up at him, boring her hatred into him.

Chad West looked stunned. His expression was a mixture of shock and anger. Brooke took the opportunity to shake his filthy hands off her. She tried to stand up, but he blocked her way.

"OK. Since you asked for it, I *will* kill you. Like I raped you because it was what you wanted. It's what every woman fantasizes about, we all know that. I only ever do what you want me to do. And now you're trying to claim that I'm the bad guy here? You deserve to die, slut." His voice was disturbingly quiet as he spoke through gritted teeth.

Brooke frowned at him as realization hit her. "You're mad." The words tumbled out of her mouth before she could stop them.

She expected a slap. He stared at her. Then he laughed. He actually laughed! A proper belly laugh as though she had made the funniest joke ever. She stared at him in disbelief as he confirmed her suspicions.

He abruptly stopped laughing and gaped at her. Pure evil stared into her eyes. She froze.

"Stand up, slut." His voice was menacing and quiet.

Brooke wasn't sure if she would actually be able to stand, but she tried anyway. Her feet throbbed as she placed them squarely on the floor, and her legs almost gave way under her body as she put her weight on them. A sharp pain in her stomach area had her doubled over in agony. She clenched her teeth, hissing at the jabbing sensation. She clung to the bench for as long as she could, trying to get her balance.

Chad moved out of her way, and she saw, for the first time, the table behind him. Her trembling started all over again when the sight of the classic bullwhip, the knife, the needles, and his old favorite, the single tail whip came into view. That sure explained the agony of her back. There was also a coil of rope and a piece of paper, which had been placed at the far end of the table. She frowned, trying to steady her breathing.

"I hope you recognize *your* letter?" he said with a hideous grin as he watched her line of sight.

She frowned again. Then the penny dropped.

"You seem to have forgotten to sign it, but then, you might want to read it first." He left her propped against the edge of the bench as he went over to retrieve the sheet of paper from the table. "You see, I had to make a few amendments due to...*unforeseen circumstances.*" He chortled wickedly as he handed her the letter.

Brooke took it from him with trembling hands.

"Take your time. Read it properly now. After all, you need to know what you're signing don't you, slut? I've just got a little job to do over here while you're reading."

She stared up at him as he went over to the table and picked up the rope. He had a vicious sneer across his face as he straightened some of it out and threw it over one of the only beams still remaining across the roof.

"Read it!" he demanded, looking across at her.

Brooke's eyes struggled to focus on the words in front of her, but she eventually managed to decipher them. Then she wished she hadn't.

TO WHOM IT MAY CONCERN

I wish to state that I, Brooke Anderson, have told lies to the police which I feel I must rectify for the sake of an innocent man, and for my own peace of mind.

I have sworn a statement which accuses Chad West of raping me on the night of OCTOBER 7, 2013. I also alleged that following this assault he beat me up and left me in a critical condition. I would like to make it known that Chad West did not perform any of these actions; I did not recognize the man who raped me as he came at me from behind in the dark. This man also beat me up. Chad West was not with me that night.

I also made other allegations to the police about Chad West which I need to address. Chad West did not whip me, beat me or in any way injure my body. The marks on my body were put there by men whom I don't know while I was a member of a BDSM club just outside Chicago. There-fore, all of these marks were made with my consent and no charges need to be made against anyone.

I sincerely apologize to the police for wasting so much of their precious time, and to Chad West, whom I have wrongfully discredited. The reason for my actions was to try to wreak revenge on him for splitting up with me. I love him so much I cannot get over losing him.

I am so ashamed of my actions that I have decided to end my own life; I cannot live with the harm I have caused to an innocent man's reputation. I hope that someday he will find it in him to forgive me.

*Signed:*___________________

*Date:*_______________

Chapter Thirteen

Brooke turned cold and she trembled with fear. Slowly she looked up to see Chad. She thought she was going to faint when she saw him standing smiling at her with his arms folded. Above his head was a noose.

"Hope you like it, sweetheart. It's a gift. I made it 'specially for you." He looked as though he had just handed her a bunch of roses.

Brooke's stomach roiled and she swallowed the bile that welled in her throat.

"You wanna try it out for size or shall we have some fun first?" He beamed at her.

This man was truly mad! She stared at him in fearful disbelief.

"What's the matter? Cat got your tongue? I see, you're speechless. It is nice, isn't it? I never get you anything but the best, do I, sweetheart?"

Her heart beat ten to the dozen, and she went from freezing cold to boiling hot in a matter of seconds. She still shook. The paper in her hand was flapping with her trembles and Chad tutted.

"Hey now. I want you signing that in your best hand-writing, d'ya hear? You need to stop being so excited or the ink'll just go everywhere. Come on, let's have some fun, then you can sign your letter and I'll be on my way. You don't want to keep me here all night, do you?"

He took her poor arm and led her to the table. She eyeballed the knife.

"Hey, I get it. Maybe you *do* want me to stay here all night with you? Is that it? You want me to make love to you all night long so you'll go with a big smile on your face?" He laughed derisively. "You really have been missing me, haven't you?"

Brooke bit her tongue hard.

"Now, let's just get these cuffs on you. Look, it's your favorite pair."

She couldn't stop the yelp that flew out of her mouth as he yanked both her arms behind her back. She was sure her right arm was broken, and she was certain he knew it too. *Fuckwad!*

He waved a pair of silver metal handcuffs in front of her face and she cringed. She recognized them. They were too small for her and bit into her skin every time he made her wear them. She recalled having to wear a watch on one wrist and a bracelet on the other for over a month whenever he let her go out because the cuffs had badly cut her wrists. He had made numerous jokes at the time about her looking as though she had tried to commit suicide.

"Don't worry, sweetheart, if they leave marks this time, the cops'll just assume you fucked up another suicide attempt before deciding to hang yourself." He laughed loudly at his own joke and callously snapped the cuffs onto her already-swollen wrists. More pain.

He leaned her forward over the table and stood behind her. Pain seared through her abdomen and her back at the same time, and she moaned desperately. She felt his body lean over hers. She could hear his breathing next to her. He was close. Too close. Her heart thudded as she anticipated his next move. He nuzzled against her ear, and she shuddered as his tongue licked it.

"Now you and I both know you're way overdue some punishment, don't we?" he murmured into her ear.

A cold chill ran through her whole body.

"*Don't* we?" he snapped.

She remained stoic. She knew him. He was like a petulant child when he didn't get what he wanted. Well, she was darned if she was going to give him what he wanted now.

He grunted angrily as he pulled her head up by the hair, tipping it back slightly. "I asked you a question, slut!"

Her eyes were forced to face the window, and her heart leaped. Two shadows were poised in the darkness, and she would recognize their physiques anywhere.

Kent's calm demeanor gave her strength, and she gazed at his gun that pointed right at the bastard behind her. Travis's determined jaw was clenched, and he too had his gun ready with Chad West in his sights.

Chad tugged at her hair again, and pain seared her head once more. Feeling weak and woozy, she forced herself to think straight as she clenched her teeth to keep from yelling. Her mind whirled with hope—all she had to do was get the fucker far enough away from her to give them a clear shot.

The bastard was getting antsier by the minute. She refused to play his game, and it irked the hell out of him. She was becoming so debilitated that it would be virtually impossible to speak to him now, anyway.

Eventually Chad took the knife and sized it up against her soft throat, which was hardly pulsating at all now. Nothing.

"I know what'll get your blood pumping," he snarled as he reached over her and grabbed the single tail from the table. He waved it menacingly in front of her face, still holding the knife to her throat.

"What do you think, slut? Don't you want to kiss your old friend?" Chad swung the tail lightly across her face, tormenting her with the potential hell he could unleash on her at any minute. Brooke held her breath, determined not to make a sound, and hoping he couldn't read the expression on her face. He huffed in disappointed exasperation. "Fuck this!"

She wasn't sure whether he had given up on the idea

of using the whip, or if he planned to use it while she hung from that dang rope. She watched tentatively, still holding her breath, as he looked around. Brooke knew he'd need to put the chair in position so he could lift her high enough to get her neck through the noose. She could feel his cold eyes staring down at her lifeless body in his arms. When she still wouldn't respond to his taunts, he simply let go of her and she plummeted unceremoniously onto the hard wooden floor.

Chad West hadn't taken one step before the first bullet pierced his chest. His startled eyes stared at the broken window where he'd see two cowboys and a sheriff, all pointing guns at him. He'd feel another stab of agony as the second bullet hit, but he'd never know anything about the third.

The door burst open and Travis ran over to the two bodies. Kent was right behind him, and they yanked the fuckwad's corpse off their girl's blood-ridden body. She felt lifeless, her soft face as beautiful as ever.

Travis could hear his heart thundering in his ears, but he couldn't hear Brooke's. He placed his fingers on her bloody throat and felt a whisper of a pulse there. Tears were streaming down his face as he turned to Kent. "She's alive—just."

He saw the tears flooding Kent's eyes as the deputy let out a sigh of relief. Travis used one hand to stroke his partner's he caressed Brooke's swollen cheek with his other. Kent turned his hand over and held his lover's tight.

"Paramedics should be here any minute. I called them as soon as I got your message on the radio. I also left the lights on the SUV so they'll find us easily," Mason spoke calmly and quietly as the two men sobbed desperately. He had already found a key in West's pocket and quickly removed the cuffs that bound Brooke's hands. Her wrists bled as he freed them.

The sheriff was as good as his word, as less than a minute later Travis could hear the siren as the ambulance pulled up as close as it could get to the wooden shack.

"Check out the girl," Mason instructed the paramedics as they ran in with their equipment. "He's dead."

The woman frowned at the sheriff, but seemed to figure he knew his stuff, so she crouched down beside Brooke. "Oxygen. I think I've got a faint pulse here." Her fingers were in the same position as Travis's had been when he detected life.

"Excuse us, gentlemen." The young man with the oxygen mask struggled to get to Brooke.

"Come on guys, over here," Mason ushered them to their feet as he stood and went over to the table. They reluctantly left Brooke's side and walked toward him.

They studied the instruments of torture that were laid out. Kent looked over at the dead body they had slung over to one side. Mason had checked that they had all done their job right, and the fuckwad was definitely no longer alive.

"No wonder she was so damn terrified of the single tail," Kent choked out, staring at the whip lying next to the corpse.

"Needles, knives...that guy must have been sick!" Travis almost shouted as anger coursed through his veins at the sight of the objects on the table. He knew the fuckwad wouldn't have learned how to use any of them properly. He scowled at the noose hanging from the battered rafter.

"That's what the cops in Chicago thought," Mason said calmly. "This is what he wanted her to sign." He picked up the sheet of paper that had been left on the bench. Blood from Brooke's hands smeared the edges.

"I'm glad I killed him." Kent's voice was calm and quiet as he stared at the body.

"Me too, buddy," Travis said with a sigh, looking over at his partner's pained expression.

"I'm glad we all killed him." The sheriff spoke through gritted teeth.

A hissing sound made them all rush over to the paramedics. "She's breathing," the woman said with a smile, apparently seeing the fear on their faces. Brooke's gorgeous body was a mass of blood, but she was alive. An oxygen mask covered her beautiful face, and tubes trailed from both her arms. A heart monitor was beeping slowly by her side.

Kent threw his arms around Travis and they both

laughed and cried at the same time. Mason patted them both on the back.

"We need to get her to the hospital right away. She needs to be fixed up to a ventilator; we're not sure how long we can keep her breathing with the equipment we've got." The medics sprung into action, sliding Brooke onto a stretcher and taking her outside.

"I'm going with her," Kent said. Travis looked crestfallen.

"You can both go in the ambulance. I'll follow on in my car and arrange for yours to be collected in the morning," Mason informed them as they followed the paramedics.

The boys nodded and climbed in behind the stretcher. It was pretty cramped with both large men in the back as well as Brooke and the medic, but there was no way Mason would let Travis drive in the state he was in.

Chapter Fourteen

"Another coffee?" Kent was on his way to the vending machine in the busy corridor near the intensive care unit at St. Paul's Community Hospital on the outskirts of Moone County.

"Thanks." Travis nodded wearily, gathering up the myriad empty plastic cups they had left strewn across the little table in front of him. He had lost count of how many drinks they had consumed in the long hours since they arrived, and sighed as he gazed at the wall clock for the umpteenth time. The short walk to the trash can gave him a chance to stretch his legs and take a look out of the large window.

"Here you go, bro." Kent handed him a fresh cup, taking the opportunity to stroke the big cowboy's arm in the process.

Travis winked and smiled at his lover. "Rain's started again." He nodded to the window and Kent looked out with him. They overlooked the small hospital parking lot, which seemed surprisingly busy for the time of night.

"At least we know the fire'll be out now," Kent said with a smirk.

Travis sighed. That was going to create a lot more work. "Hal's calling in the insurance company for us. We should have the loss adjusters around anytime now."

"What about the horses?" Kent bit his lip.

"Frank Buchanan's taken them in until we can get the work done on the stables. I sure hope the insurance company doesn't drag their heels. I want those beauties home as soon as I can." Travis frowned.

They had both made use of the hospital's payphones earlier. It had afforded them peace of mind as well as something to do to kill the boredom of waiting around. Both guys did their best to take each other's minds off the horrors of the earlier incident and the fear of the outcome of their poor girl, who had been rushed into the OR as soon as they had arrived.

"Mason's asking around about the fuckwad—someone's got to have seen something. I wanna know how the hell he made the connection between us and Brooke. He must have either been there last night or he saw her at the ranch when she had that accident," Kent mused, still gazing out of the rain-soaked window.

Travis arched an eyebrow. "Assuming it *was* an accident."

Kent frowned. "If the fucker had been involved would he have left her there?"

"He left her for dead after he raped her."

"I suppose if he thought she was a goner he *could* have just left her."

"Well one thing's for sure; he didn't go down and check on her. I'd have seen his tracks." Travis pursed his lips.

"Thank fuck he's dead!"

"Amen to that, buddy."

Kent sighed and snuggled into Travis, who put a comforting arm around him. Even as deputy sheriff, Kent didn't like to have to kill anyone, but this afternoon had sure been the exception. They stared in silence as the rain pelted the large window in front of them. His thoughts were still at the shack, his heart in the OR.

"I thought he'd never move away from her," Kent said at last, recalling their agonizing wait at the broken window of the shack, guns poised, desperate for the fuckwad to take a step away from their girl so they could kill him. "Our girl played a damn smart game back there, not reacting to him. She must have known it would piss the hell out of him."

"I was afraid she'd die in his arms before we could get to her," Travis said ruefully.

They squeezed each other tight, still staring vacantly out of the window into the darkness.

They stood there for nearly an hour before something caught Kent's eye.

"Mason's back."

The black SUV pulled up under a streetlamp in the

parking lot, and their friend climbed out. He looked older and weary, and Kent guessed he hadn't gotten any sleep yet, either. They met him by the entrance.

"Any news?" Mason Bains studied their fearful expressions.

Travis shook his head. "She's still in surgery."

Mason nodded. "Anywhere to get a coffee around here?"

Kent guessed he had news for them that could hardly be discussed in the busy foyer of the hospital.

"Down here." Kent led them back down the corridor that led to the ICU. He bought them all coffee from the machine before Travis indicated a small empty seating area off the main corridor.

"Well, the body's been recovered and Hal drove your truck back to the ranch. He insisted on coming with me back to the shack when I took the coroner up there. Good job, too. He reckons he might have seen the evil bastard at the gig last night. Thinks he might have been talking to Rich Buchanan. I'll go up there later and check that out." Mason sighed as they all got comfortable.

"Fucking hell!" Travis was livid. "He was right under our noses and we didn't know it? How the hell did that happen?"

"Oh he was a clever fucker." Mason was speaking through gritted teeth. "Apparently the cops thought they'd caught up with him a couple of times, but he always managed to slip through the net. Had a lot of connections, I heard, although a lot of his so-called friends deserted him once they found out he was wanted for rape and attempted murder. Even scum have their principles!

"I spoke to his mom. She was shocked and…well, relieved to hear he was dead. She'd already told the cops that she thought he was mentally ill. Some of the things he's done would make your toes curl. The family disowned him years ago when they found out he was dealing in drugs. The cops have been trying to pin something on him for ages but could never quite get the slippery bastard. Seems he had some friends in some very high places. High in rank as well as high on dope."

"So he was supplying the rich and mighty? That figures." Kent scorned.

"Anyway, it turns out Brooke had no choice but to furnish the cops with all the information she had on him. No one expected her to make it through more than a couple of days after she came out of the coma following that attack. She thought she had nothing to lose. When she started to recover, they had a guard sat outside her hospital room twenty-four hours a day in case he showed up. They promised her protection at home too. That's where they messed up. They checked that the apartment was safe, so she went to fetch her stuff. Unfortunately there was some mix-up, and the cops who were supposed to look out for her got deployed on a massive job which turned out to be a hoax. By the time they got to the apartment, she'd gone. By their reckoning, West had left town around the same time." Mason rubbed his hands over his tired face.

"She said the cops let her down. That's why she wouldn't trust the law. That's why she couldn't trust *me*." Kent sighed sadly.

"But she *did* trust you, buddy. You heard what Stella Montgomery said. She tried to call us because she wanted to *be* with us. She realized she'd been wrong about everything. She wanted to join our family. She loves us." Travis put a hand over Kent's as he spoke softly to him. Kent leaned his forehead against his lover's.

"The cops reckon he probably had something to do with the hoax call but haven't been able to prove anything yet," Mason said quietly.

Travis's head shot up. "Just like he set fire to the stables to stop us from getting to her."

Mason nodded. "That's exactly what we thought, son."

"Bastard! If I hadn't already killed him, I'd do it right now," Kent seethed.

Travis caught sight of a woman in scrubs walking down the main corridor and leapt to his feet. She was a nurse who had spoken to them when they first arrived. He caught up with her in a couple of his massive strides.

"Yes, sir, the doctor will be out to see you shortly," she replied curtly to his inquiry.

"Have you seen her? Is she OK?" he couldn't help but ask.

The nurse bit her lip. "She sustained multiple injuries

and is still on a ventilator to help with her breathing. The doctor will be able to give you more details."

"Have they finished in there? Is she coming out?"

The nurse sighed. "They're finishing up now. She'll be taken to the ICU in a while, sir. The doctor will be able to tell you whether or not you'll be allowed to go and see her."

"Thank you, ma'am, I much appreciate your help." Travis nodded as he turned to go.

"Er—Mr. Beaumont."

"Ma'am?" Travis took a step nearer to her, his eyebrows raised quizzically.

She bit her lip nervously as she looked up at him. "I have to know. She's sustained multiple severe lacerations across her body. The person who did this...?"

"He's dead, ma'am. I shot him," Travis replied.

She let out a sigh of relief and smiled at him. "Thank you, sir." She turned and hurried off up the corridor.

Kent was waiting for him when he returned to the seating area. "Any news?"

Travis relayed the message.

"She's alive. That's the main thing," Mason stated, seeing the disappointment on their faces.

"Yes, sir, you're right." Travis sighed and leaned back in his seat.

It was nearly an hour later when the doctor came out to speak to them. He must have been in his fifties and was still dressed in scrubs. "Are you Brooke Anderson's next of kin?"

Kent opened his eyes. He hadn't been sleeping as such, just resting. "We're the nearest she's got, sir," he replied, standing up to shake his hand.

The doctor looked over to the sheriff, who nodded his affirmation. "Very well. I'm Dr. Shearan, Brooke's consultant. They will be taking her out of surgery very soon and she'll be looked after in our intensive care unit, just down the corridor. I have to warn you that she is still in a critical condition and is using a ventilator to help her breathe."

"Will she be all right, Dr. Shearan?" Travis stood next to Kent, trembling slightly.

"The honest answer is that I'm afraid I don't know. Apart from a broken arm, several fractured ribs, and obvious lacerations to her body—some of which were very severe, I should warn you—we also had to check out some renal trauma and a damaged spleen. We managed to stem the internal bleeding, but now it's a waiting game to see if we've done enough. We've scanned her head, which sustained some severe trauma in the car crash, and we've detected some slight swelling, but no bleeding. We just have to continue to monitor her for now and see how she fares. We won't actually know the full extent of the damage until she recovers consciousness." Dr. Shearan frowned as he spoke.

Kent clutched Travis's arm. He felt cold and weary, but that was nothing compared to the fear and anxiety that gripped him by the throat.

"How's her back, doctor?" Mason Bains was studying the man's face and apparently didn't like what he saw.

The doctor cleared his throat and looked over to the sheriff, who had just stood up to join them.

"It looked to me like she had been whipped long and hard. The lacerations were quite deep in places, but what about internal injury?" Mason's voice was calm and clear.

Travis and Kent both turned and stared at the doctor. What wasn't he telling them?

Dr. Shearan took a deep breath. "We checked her out for spinal cord injury and cervical dislocation or injury. The scan didn't show much, although there seems to be some swelling around the lower lumbar region. Her legs appear very bruised, but we couldn't detect any thrombosis at this time. We're going to keep a close eye on things in case something emerges in the next twenty-four hours or so. Also, her neck has been placed in a cervical collar for the time being. We believe she has whiplash injuries, and the tissues around the neck area are severely swollen."

"She must have been in agony." Kent had tears pricking at the corners of his eyes. Travis wrapped a strong arm around him, as much for his own comfort as for his lover's.

"Can the boys see her, doctor?" Mason was clearly shocked but maintained a professional demeanor.

"Just for a few moments after we get her settled. I'll send a nurse through in a while," Dr. Shearan replied and set off toward the ICU.

"How about you boys get freshened up a little before you go see her? I'll see if I can find us some sandwiches or something while we wait." Mason smiled kindly at the teary-eyed guys, and they nodded gratefully before heading for the men's room.

"I look like hell!" Travis declared in his lazy drawl as he caught sight of himself in the mirror. He immediately removed his shirt while running a basin full of warm water.

Kent stood next to him. The men's room was small but beautifully clean. He looked at his own reflection and sighed. "It's a good thing she won't be able to see us. She won't want either of us looking like this." He stripped off his own shirt and began to wash.

"I'm not sure about this soap," Travis said with a grin as he smelled the pile of foam he had just dispensed.

"Let's see." Kent leaned over to sniff the substance in his hand just as Travis lifted it, planting a pile of sweet-smelling froth right in his face.

Kent stared at his lover, stunned for a second. That was the last thing he'd expected. Travis let out a whoop of laughter that echoed around the empty room.

With a giggle, Kent scooped a handful of water from the hand basin and splashed it over Travis's naked chest.

Travis raised his eyebrows as he laughed again and returned the favor. Soon the boys were giggling like schoolchildren and splashing water all over each other. After a few minutes, Travis reached over to Kent and, with a wet hand, washed his lover's face using the soap he had deposited there earlier. He felt Kent's stubble with his rough hands and he toyed with it lovingly. He took more water and rinsed the soap away before leaning in to kiss his lover's soft, full lips. His tongue lapped at the seam before gliding into Kent's welcoming mouth. He felt Kent's hands run down his chest, over his shoulders, and then down his back as they squeezed each other in a warm embrace.

Kent could feel his lover's heat as their tongues danced slowly together, and their bodies pressed against each other, melting into each other as though they had become one person. Time seemed to stand still as their love and care for each other emanated through their minds, each engulfing the other in their adulation.

Gradually they withdraw their mouths and loosened their grip on each other's body. They stared into each other's eyes, sharing unspoken emotions. Neither spoke as they smiled to each other before resuming their wash up. It was a relief to feel clean again as well as having relieved some of their tension for a few light hearted moments. They both sighed as they pulled on their shirts and ran their wet hands through their tousled hair.

"I look better already," Travis said with a grin as he studied himself in the mirror. His eyes were a little red and baggy, and his cheeks looked quite drawn, but he felt better.

Kent laughed and Travis watched him study his own reflection. He had lines on his cheeks where he had been leaning against the side of the chair resting, and his eyes looked pale and weary. Whiskers had grown on his usually clean-shaven jaw, and he looked a little rugged.

"Perfect." Kent grinned and they went back to find the sheriff.

Mason had come up trumps with the food. He had placed a selection of vacuum-packed sandwiches on the table along with several bags of potato chips. There was more coffee and even doughnuts.

"Wow, Dad, thanks for the picnic." Kent smiled approvingly as he sat down.

"I can still fire you, you know," Mason grumbled jokingly.

"Oh, please don't. I'd have to suffer him on the ranch full-time if you did that!" Travis grinned as he tucked into a chicken-salad sandwich.

"You two look a lot better." Mason smiled at them as he passed around the chips.

"We've got to look good for our girl," Travis replied.

"How long do you think they'll keep us waiting?" Kent was peering down the corridor as he picked a slice of tomato from his sandwich.

"It shouldn't be too long now," Mason said calmly.

Travis's stomach rumbled loudly. He glanced over at

Mason's watch. "We've been going nearly twenty-four hours without eating. How the hell did that happen?"

"I think food was the last thing on our minds," Kent replied with a sigh.

Travis placed a comforting hand on his lover's. "We'll see her soon, buddy."

Kent smiled at Travis's cheerful face. He loved his partner's optimism.

"That girl's gonna need a lot of taking care of after all this," Mason declared as he gulped his coffee.

"I reckon we're up to the task," Travis said with a grin.

"We haven't done such a good job up until now," Kent remarked ruefully.

"What're you talking about, buddy? We killed the motherfucker who was making her life hell. We've enabled her to start living again instead of running all the time. I reckon we've done all right there." Travis gave Kent a playful punch on the arm.

Kent shook his head and smiled. "Well now, I suppose if you put it like that..."

"Dr. Shearan said you can see her now," a young nurse interrupted their banter, and they both shot to their feet.

Their jokey demeanor vanished as they walked reverently into the ICU. Brooke was in a side room, hooked up to numerous machines that beeped and blipped a merry chorus. A big computer-type machine was on the wall above her head with numbers flashing and lines of light flickering up and down. The room was dark and warm, and a nurse stood by the bedside.

Kent was the first though the door and he stopped abruptly when he caught sight of her. She was lying so still and lifeless. The cervical collar surrounded her neck, and a large white bandage was tied around her head. Her arms lay over the white bedcover. One was in a cast; the other had a cannula fitted with several tubes running from it.

"Just a few minutes," the nurse whispered as she made way for them and headed toward the door.

Kent's heart pounded and he took deep breaths to steady his nerves as he neared the top of the bed. He stared at her soft, angelic face. A large dressing covered her left cheek, while the rest of her skin was a mass of cuts and bruises. Her lower face was concealed by a small mask with a tube which protruded from her lips, covered by a full mask over her mouth and nose. It was connected by a long tube to the ventilator that worked its magic at the side of the bed. She looked so fragile, so beautiful. A large lump welled in the back of his throat and he took deep breaths to keep his tears at bay.

Travis followed Kent into the room and immediately made his way across to the other side of her bed. He shook his head in disbelief as he took in the sight of their beloved woman, who looked helpless and totally dependent on the people and machines that surrounded her. He stared at her eyes. They didn't even flicker. Travis's face went bright red, and he started blinking rapidly as tears threatened his eyes.

Both men stared in silence, not even daring to reach out and touch her. Kent didn't have the heart to tell Travis their ordeal might not yet be over. He couldn't stop thinking about what Mason had said—Chad had friends. Sure, most had abandoned him, but there had to be at least one creep out there who wouldn't be happy with what had gone down in Moone County. Kent gazed down at Brooke.

This would not happen again.

Chapter Fifteen

The next few days passed painfully slowly. Although Brooke's vital signs improved and she was taken off the ventilator, she failed to open her eyes. Kent prolonged his leave from work, and the boys took turns staying with their girl all through the long days and nights. At first they had spent all their time waiting around outside, only being allowed to pop in to see her for a few minutes, but now they were sitting quietly at her bedside whenever it was feasible.

"Don't look so down." Dr. Shearan caught Kent's expression as he sat by her bedside on the afternoon of the fifth day.

"She doesn't seem to want to wake up," Kent said sadly.

"Her body and mind went through a lot of trauma," Dr. Shearan explained, picking up his notes. "It needs time to recover. While she's resting, she's giving them both time to heal. It looks like it's working well too." He was studying the pages in front of him and then looked down at her. "Her kidney and spleen appear to be working satisfactorily. I would expect them to recover completely."

"She won't have to go on dialysis or anything then?" Kent perked up slightly.

Dr. Shearan shook his head. "No, her kidney was only bruised." He flipped the page in his notes. Then he stood over Brooke and peered at her intently.

"Is everything OK, Doctor?" Kent hardly dared ask.

The consultant was quiet for a minute before straightening up and smiling at him. "Oh yes. I would expect her to wake up before too long. Most of her swellings are going down now, and we haven't detected anything which causes concern."

Kent beamed. "How soon before she wakes up? Should I call Travis?" He was practically jumping out of the chair.

Dr. Shearan chuckled. "Not yet, son. Your friend was here all night, I think he needs to rest himself. Give it a couple more hours and I'll check on her again. Then you can call him if things are still on the up."

Kent sat down again a little reluctantly. He was still holding Brooke's hand. He gazed down at her pale face. The dressing on her cheek had been reduced to a slightly smaller one than she first had, and the swelling around her cuts wasn't quite so severe. She still had the large bandage around her head and the cervical collar. She looked beautiful.

"I'll be back later. Make sure you get some rest yourself before she wakes up." Dr. Shearan smiled kindly as he left the room.

Kent sighed. He stroked her hand and sat back in what must have been the most uncomfortable chair on God's earth. Being a large, muscular man, he found it a bit of a squeeze just to sit down, and then the arms dug into his hips. The back was straight and upright and just the wrong height. Whenever he dozed off, he woke with a crick in his neck. It was worth the discomfort to be able to stay with Brooke, though. The first day or two spent roaming the corridor outside had seemed endless, and not being able to see her nearly killed him.

One of the nurses appeared with a cup of tea for him. The staff didn't mind their company one bit.

"Thank you." Kent smiled at her and watched her blush.

"She's looking better." The woman nodded over to Brooke.

"Dr. Shearan reckons she'll be waking up before too long," Kent informed her before taking a long sip of his tea.

The nurse smiled. "She'll need a lot of looking after when she gets out."

"She's going to get that, all right. We won't let her lift a finger once she gets home. She'll get all the rest she needs. She won't be allowed to move a muscle."

The nurse laughed. "I think the physical therapist will have something to say about that. Once that collar comes off, she needs to be moving her head again, and those legs will cramp up without a bit of exercise now and then."

"Well, all right, as long as it's doctor's orders," Kent relented with a grin.

"That poor girl won't know what's hit her when you two get her home. I'll bet she's used to her independence. You'll have to be careful, you know." The nurse chuckled.

"Don't you worry; we'll take care of everything." Kent had a self-satisfied grin on his face as he sipped his tea.

The nurse shook her head, smiling, and left the room.

The staff was all well aware of the boys' plans to take Brooke home and look after her on the ranch once she was better. Most of them were a little jealous, truth be told. Brooke was going to need a lot of help with her recovery, though, and the guys were determined they would be the ones to give it to her. They would give her the world on a silver plate if they could.

Kent finished his tea and took one more look at their sleeping beauty before settling as best he could for a nap. The room was warm and quiet except for a machine that insisted on bleeping all the time, and he soon drifted off.

~

Brooke was gradually becoming aware of muffled sounds around her. Light flickered into her eyes as they slowly fluttered open. Pain throbbed through her body, though she couldn't pinpoint where it was worse. She felt heavy and tired, and very peaceful. As she eventually managed to open her eyes fully, she realized she was lying in a dark room. An incessant beeping sound invaded her ears, and a clean, sterile smell assaulted her nose. The world seemed to be moving in slow motion. She was aware of the presence of somebody—or some bodies—near her, but she felt that she was a million miles away from them. Her brain was a heap of mush, and just moving her eyes was almost too much effort.

A dark shadow moved over her and she smelled a familiar scent. She knew she liked the faint aroma but couldn't remember what it was. A warm, soft hand was holding hers, and she forced herself to move one of her fingers slightly. A soft, breathy voice murmured near her face, and she felt an aura of calmness and safety. She sighed.

"Brooke, baby, can you hear me?"

Words permeated her brain and danced inside her head before forming a coherent sentence. When they finally made sense, she stared into the darkness at the man who had spoken to her, and through the blur she saw a face she loved gradually materialize. She slowly licked her lips to force her mouth to open and strained her sore throat to push out a small sound.

It was enough to make him smile. A dazzling smile

full of hope, care, and love beamed down at her. She felt something deep inside her glow warm, and suddenly the pain didn't seem so bad. She stared up at the big green eyes twinkling down at her. She didn't have the energy to smile or speak or move a single muscle, but it was OK. He seemed happy for them just to gaze at each other.

More muffled sounds encroached on their reverie as nurses and doctors flitted around the room. She felt bereft when the big, warm hand left hers and someone clipped something onto her finger while wrapping a cold cuff around her arm. Voices were becoming louder as more bodies crowded her, and she slowly managed to make out the shapes of people around her.

Brooke couldn't move her head; her neck felt as though it was caught in a vise. Her eyes began darting around wildly as her peace was shattered, and she felt herself start to panic with the mayhem surrounding her.

"It's all right, baby. I'm still here." A waft of Diesel aftershave steadied her nerves as Kent's gentle voice whispered to her from the opposite side of the bed. He had just moved out of the way of the nurses but hadn't left her. Brooke's whole body started to relax again, and she focused on the handsome face that came into her line of vision.

Muted voices surrounded her, but she wasn't interested in them. She just concentrated on the one whispering soothingly into her ear. The warm glow returned to her insides, and she felt a deep sigh escape her lips.

"Travis is on his way, baby, he won't be long now."

She heard Kent whisper to her, and another hot ember radiated from somewhere deep inside her. Brooke actually felt her lips move into a slight smile, and was relieved that Kent saw it too. He chuckled deep in his throat. She remembered how much she loved that sound.

The crowd around them finally dissipated and a nurse leaned in to speak to Kent. "Just a few more minutes, Deputy, she needs some rest."

Kent nodded to her as he stroked Brooke's face gently. The soothing motion and the softness of his hand comforted and warmed her, and her eyelids began to droop.

"Shh," he whispered as she fought the sleep that threatened to engulf her. She wanted to stay with him, but it was too much. Peacefulness surrounded her. A feeling of calm and safety, and knowing her men weren't far away were all she needed. The sensation enveloped her like a warm blanket as she finally relented and allowed herself to sleep.

Kent sat by her side for a short while before the nurse returned and ushered him out. "She'll be asleep for a while now. Go get yourself a coffee. Mr. Beaumont's just arrived, and the doctor wants to fill you in on a few things." She smiled at him, and he reluctantly stood up, kissed Brooke's soft, swollen cheek, and went to find his lover.

Travis was running up the corridor toward him. Kent headed him off before he rushed into the little side room to see Brooke. "She's gone back to sleep," Kent whispered, holding on to Travis's arm.

"Holy cow, I only just got here!" Travis looked crestfallen as Kent veered him toward the vending machine.

"The nurse reckons she'll be resting for a bit, but you'll probably see her a bit later on. In the meantime, the doctor wants a word with us." Kent handed him a cup of coffee and they went to look out of the big window in the corridor while they waited.

"Did she say anything? Is she OK?" Travis's mind was racing.

Kent grinned. "She wasn't up to talking."

Travis looked disappointed.

"I told her you were on your way, though, and she managed a smile."

Travis beamed. "For real?"

Kent nodded. "I got the impression she was trying to stay awake till you got here, but she just couldn't quite make it."

Travis nuzzled against his lover, and they enjoyed a coffee-flavored kiss before footsteps alerted them that Dr. Shearan was on his way.

"What's the news, Doc?" Travis got straight to the point.

"Well, it's good, actually. Your girl seems to be

showing all the right signs. We'll be taking the cervical collar off in a couple of days to see how she goes. Her spleen and kidney seem to be behaving themselves too. We need to do a few more tests once she's fully awake to check out possible spinal problems, though. The swelling in her lumbar region is still concerning us, but don't worry too much at this stage; it could be just taking its time to heal. It's still very early days yet." Dr. Shearan sounded quite optimistic, which raised Travis's spirits even more.

"Can I see her? I want to be there when she wakes up." Travis was a little peeved that he had missed out.

"Of course. The nurses will be with her for a short while now, though, but you're welcome to come back in, say, half an hour and sit with her quietly." Dr. Shearan smiled.

"Thank you, sir." Travis grinned back.

Kent nodded to the doctor as he went back to his duties.

"Happy now?" Kent teased his partner.

"Hell no. I should've run a few more of them dang red lights to get here." Travis shook his head thoughtfully.

"You should not have! I'll have your guts for garters if I find you doing that, d'you hear me?" Mason appeared behind them, giving Travis the shock of his life.

He turned around and grinned. "You'll have to catch me first, Sheriff."

Mason let out a deep laugh. "In that dang truck of yours? No problem, son."

Travis screwed up his handsome face a little. "You might have a point there, actually, Sheriff."

Mason Bains was still giggling when the three men went to sit down with their coffees.

"So, are you longing to get me back to work yet, boss?" Kent grinned at the sheriff, who had insisted that his deputy was no good to him while his mind was constantly in the ICU of their local hospital. Kent had been ordered to prolong his leave of absence until he was ready to return to the job, and he wasn't about to complain. He and Travis had kept vigil at Brooke's bedside nonstop since she was admitted.

"Nope. You take as long as you need. I hear she just woke up today?" Mason smiled.

"Yep. She was so beautiful. I can't wait till she starts talking again. I just know it's gonna be right this time." Kent had an unusual optimism about him this evening that couldn't fail to make the other two smile.

"Well, that's good." Mason seemed genuinely pleased for them.

"Travis, Wyatt Hennessey told me he's planning on bringing in a couple of new guys to help out with the building work for your new stable block. I've managed to check one of them out but I'm still trying to get the gen on the other. He's not come up on the radar, so that's good, but I can't seem to find anything on him at all. I've still got some irons in the fire, so to speak, but Wyatt needs to know if you're happy for him to start up there while we're still looking." Mason frowned as he drank his coffee.

Travis sighed. "Well now, I suppose if Wyatt's happy to employ him, I'd be happy to have him do the job. Lord knows I need all the help I can get up there. As soon as the insurance give us the go-ahead I want that work started right away. I don't want Frank Buchanan getting too attached to my horses."

"All right, then. I'll let Wyatt know. I'm still gonna keep checking, though. People without a past give me the willies." Mason finished his drink and put his cup in the trash can. "You let me know if there's any news on your girl. Some of us still have work to do." He grinned as he left them.

A nurse approached the boys soon after the sheriff went. "You can go in now if you like. She's still asleep."

They didn't need telling twice. Both guys shot to their feet and headed for the little side room.

"She is so beautiful." Travis sighed as he took a seat by her side, taking her soft hand in his.

"D'you think she'll still want to come live with us when she gets out?" Kent sat at her other side, stroking her hair.

"Stella said she'd have come up that day if we'd answered the goddam phone. I reckon she still would."

"She thinks we didn't answer it 'cause we didn't want her. I hope we can convince her that's not true."

"She'll understand, buddy, trust me."

Kent smiled. Travis knew he trusted him with his life, his whole future. They had always spoken about wanting a girl to join them—they both had needs that only a woman could fulfill—but since Kathy had dumped them, he had begun to think it would never happen. Kent was fast approaching thirty and was ready to really settle down.

Travis was gazing at Brooke's lovely face when her eyelids began to flutter. His heart sped up and he moved forward a little. He couldn't get close enough to this gorgeous woman.

"Hi, darlin'." He kept his voice low and a massive grin crossed his face when she opened her big blue eyes and stared straight at him. He watched her mouth twitch into a small smile, and his insides glowed like red-hot coals.

"Hi." Her voice was not much more than a strangled whisper, but it was more than enough.

She was gazing into his face, and he stroked the back of her hand as he leaned forward even more.

"You're gonna be OK now, d'ya hear? You're safe. We're gonna look after you." Travis spoke quietly and clearly. He could obviously see her concentrating on his face and his words.

Poor love, Kent thought, she must be totally confused waking up here like this.

Her mouth twitched again, and she gave a very faint nod as her eyes gradually started to close.

"Hey, baby. You just get better soon, OK? We'll take care of everything." Kent leaned forward and whispered to her softly.

Her head moved slightly and he saw her try to face him, so he moved even closer. She had a flicker of a smile on her face. Her head nodded ever so slightly as her heavy eyelids fell closed once more.

The guys sat staring at her for a few minutes. She appeared to be still smiling, and looked so peaceful and angelic it was hard to tear their eyes away.

A warm flame of hope burned brightly within Kent's body, and he knew their dream was on the precipice of coming true.

Chapter Sixteen

It was a couple of long weeks before the boys were actually allowed to take their girl home. They had cleaned the ranch house from top to bottom, and Kent had locked the door to the playroom.

"Looks like Ty's gonna have to run his place without us from now on," he said with a sigh.

"I know giving up the BDSM's gonna be hard, but it'll be worth it to keep our girl feeling safe and happy, don't you reckon?" Travis pouted.

"You're right there, bro. Well, I think it's about time we went and got her, don't you?"

They had both dressed in smart shirts and tight jeans, and even dusted off their boots and hats to try to look presentable enough to make Brooke proud. Nothing was going to spoil her homecoming.

~

Their grooming efforts certainly paid off when Brooke's face lit up appreciatively as they walked into her side room. She had been moved from the ICU over a week ago and now occupied a small room off one of the main wards. The intention had been to keep her quiet and rested, but she hadn't been able to resist popping out to make friends with the ladies on the main ward once she was feeling better. Their little minx had furnished the boys with a whole manner of tidbits of information about what the other ladies were in for and for how long —as well as some rather spicy snippets about their private lives. No one bothered to keep secrets in Moone!

"You look lovely," she told them as she reached up for a kiss with Travis. He didn't disappoint. He took her gently around her soft waist and devoured her mouth in a long, loving kiss. His Armani surrounded her in a sensual cloud, and she breathed him in as his hot tongue danced with hers.

"Hi, baby." Kent threw her a dazzling smile as Travis stood back, and her good arm automatically reached for his shoulder. He leaned down and gave her the soft, hedonistic kiss she craved from him. His soft arms enveloped her and she smelled his lighter scent, Diesel, as he gently lapped at her lips and explored her hot mouth.

"The doctor's happy for her to leave now. I just need to give you these." An older-looking nurse handed Travis a bag of medication and some sheets of instructions for her care.

"Thank you, ma'am." Travis doffed his hat politely as

he took them from her. The nurse smiled, blushing slightly.

"Have you got everything?" Kent asked when he finally let go of Brooke.

"There's only this." She picked up a small wash bag he had bought her when she was first admitted. It had everything she would need in it; he had made sure of that. He smiled as he took it from her.

"Well, I guess that's us all set, then," Travis said as he headed for the door, swinging his free arm over her shoulder. Kent put his free arm around her too, and she felt their warmth as she was placed in a sandwich of their love.

"Yes, I've said good-bye to everyone." She smiled up at Travis, who grinned back.

"Thank the Lord for that. We could have been here another couple of hours by the time you made your rounds." Travis squeezed her gently as he chuckled.

Brooke giggled up at him. The boys seemed to understand her need to be with people. She had realized how lonely she had been while on the run, never being able to really get to know anyone in case it worked against her. Now she felt relaxed and able to start making friends again. She felt like a new woman.

"How is everything?" she asked as she sat between them on the bench seat of the pickup. Even the truck had been cleaned for the occasion.

"Good. The men are getting on well with the stables.

As long as the weather holds out, they should be able to start on the roof soon." Travis smiled.

"When will we get the rest of the horses back?" Brooke was looking forward to being able to go riding again.

"Probably another couple of weeks. Frank Buchanan's doing a great job looking after them. We've still got a few which were in the old stables, so there's plenty to keep the guys occupied."

"But you won't be helping them for a while, baby, so don't you go getting any ideas," Kent interjected, as if reading her mind.

Brooke pouted. "But I've been itching to get on and do something. Have you any idea how bored I've been stuck in that bed these last couple of weeks? I'm going stir-crazy here."

The boys chuckled. They knew only too well how bored she'd been in that hospital bed. As soon as she'd had the cervical collar removed, she'd started reading anything and everything. Once they'd found her reading her own medical notes. It was only meant to give herself something to do, but it had her in tears when she realized just how bad off she'd been. After that, they'd brought her every magazine in the shop and even joined the local library so they could furnish her with something different to keep her busy.

Once she was up on her feet, it was a different story. She'd made friends with everyone on the main section and would have been down to the next ward if Travis hadn't returned from a short break one day to find her roaming the corridor.

"The doctor said you could come home now, provided you still got adequate rest," Travis reminded her as he turned into the ranch.

"But I can't sit around doing nothing." She moaned as she sat forward to study the damage to the stable block. "Oh my God!" Her blood ran cold and she stared at the sight in front of them.

The fire had eaten away most of the block and rendered the remains unusable, so the whole thing had to be demolished. There were several men working on building a new block, which they had positioned a little farther from the main house for safety.

"When you told me what Chad had done, I thought..." Brooke's voice was small and shaky.

"Don't you even think about it, darlin'. Look, the insurance company's buying me a brand-new stable complete with all sorts of equipment. That fuckwad did me a favor in the end!" Travis tried to sound cheerful, but she could sense a shard of anger at the sound of Chad.

"Come on, let's get you inside. Time you had your feet up, I reckon." Kent swiftly changed the subject as Travis pulled up right outside the house.

Brooke took a deep breath and, with one handsome hunk holding her on each side, made her way into the house. Her legs were still a little wobbly; Chad had wrenched them to get her free of the wreckage without any thought as to her welfare, and the swelling in her lumbar region had only added to the pains that shot up and down her thighs. She felt a tinge of sadness at the way she had left this place just a few short weeks ago—terrified and devastated.

She looked up at Kent. He was gorgeous. His jeans were tight enough to accentuate his shapely butt, and he had one of his best shirts on; he loved those shirts. His face was confident and kind, and she now realized there was no way he would harm anyone with or without a single tail. Well, anyone except the fuckwad who had been on the receiving end of his bullet. She knew Kent had been the first to fire and she knew why. It had been his gift to her.

"Hey now, what's all this?" The deputy was the first to notice the tears streaming down her face as she entered the living room.

Travis looked nervously around the room he had spent so much time polishing and scrubbing ready for her arrival. "Is something wrong, darlin'?"

Brooke shook her head, unable to speak.

They led her to the large sofa and sat her down with one of them either side of her. Kent drew her head to his heaving chest while Travis snuggled into her other side with a strong arm draped around her. They let her cry while they gently soothed and stroked her.

The boys had been warned that she would be very emotional following her trauma, and the counselor who had been seeing her at the hospital was scheduled to visit tomorrow. It would be a while before the horrors of the recent events would fade into the back of her mind, and she had to spend this time facing them head-on and dealing with them as best she could. Dr. Shearan had assured the guys that with their help and understanding, accompanied by the follow-up of the trained counselor, she *would* recover mentally as well as physically. It was just a matter of time.

Brooke stirred about an hour later and realized she had fallen asleep enveloped in her two guys. She could smell a mixture of their aftershave as she slowly came to her senses. She could hear Kent's strong heart pumping rhythmically in her ear and felt Travis's warm body against her other side. His muscular arm held her protectively, and there was something hard jabbing into her thigh. Oh my God! She sniggered as she realized that Travis's rock-hard cock was making its presence well and truly felt.

"Hi, baby." Kent sensed her waking and nuzzled her soft hair, murmuring quietly.

Brooke lifted her head and both guys started to move slowly. "I'm sorry." She flushed a little at the recognition that she had just cried herself to sleep on them both.

They snuggled closer to her, and she heard a chuckle from deep in Travis's throat. "Don't sweat it, darlin'. Kent makes a lovely pillow. What with that and his boring line of conversation, I fall asleep on him all the time."

Kent huffed and shook his head. "See what I have to put up with, baby? I'm so glad I've got *you* here to appreciate me." He smiled down at her, and she nudged closer into his soft body with a giggle.

"I can see I'm gonna have my work cut out for me with you two." She shook her head in mock despair, causing her blonde curls to tumble around her face.

"Think you can cope with us, darlin'?" Travis raised a sexy eyebrow at her, and she just knew he wasn't just referring to their banter. She flushed and a small fire smoldered inside her. A vision of being in bed with them both—with that hard cock—flashed through her mind, rendering her speechless.

When she didn't answer, Kent turned to face her, a slightly worried expression on his face.

Brooke looked from Kent's concern to Travis's wicked grin and just knew she was in trouble. "I reckon I can handle it," she said with a grin.

Kent's face relaxed and he beamed. Travis's eyes twinkled with mirth. They snuggled even closer. Brooke loved being in between them. This was where she belonged.

"Well, I best get the dinner dished up. I hope you like beef stew, Brooke? I've had it simmering all day."

Brooke grinned, suddenly realizing how hungry she was. "I love it. Can I help?"

She was already trying to stand up when Travis caught hold of her. "Not today, darlin'. Today you sit and get waited on. When you're better you can get up and do things, but not now." He held her firmly as Kent chuckled and headed for the kitchen.

"Travis, I'm fine, really. They wouldn't have let me come home if I wasn't, now would they?" she protested.

A massive smile filled Travis's face. Now what could have gotten him so happy? It hit her—she'd referred to this place as her home.

"I think now you're home you're gonna have to behave yourself, darlin'. No more of that running around nonsense you tried in that hospital. You had the nurses worried sick every time they came and found your bed empty. There's no bored women around here for you to gossip to. You just have to sit quiet and do as you're told. You got that?"

Brooke gasped as she realized her pussy had just clenched. Travis had a pleasant smile on his face, but his voice had been deep and authoritative. That voice was going to be her undoing! She closed her eyes momentarily and realized she was flushing as her whole body heated up. The smolder deep inside her had grown into a fully-fledged flame, and she swallowed hard as she conceded that she was, in fact, really turned-on.

With a deep breath she opened her eyes. He was staring at her expectantly. How was she supposed to answer that? Her dry mouth opened and she whispered her assent. "Yes, sir."

They both gawked at each other. Where the hell did sir come from? Her horrified gape met his astonished approval. With a crimson blush, she looked down at her trembling hand fidgeting in her lap with the denim of her jeans. She was sure the other hand would be shaking just as much had it not been anchored in place with a fat heap of plaster of Paris.

She felt his strong finger under her chin as he lifted her face up to look at him. She strained her eyes to look elsewhere, but he waited patiently until they settled on his. His big brown eyes had turned almost black, and he wore the most delicious expression. "Thank you," he whispered close to her lips. The fire inside her shot up like a rocket. His approval suddenly meant everything to her, though she didn't know why.

Travis's lips met hers. They were soft at first, licking at her gently before delving into her hot mouth. His tongue was warm and wet as it danced with hers to a melody only they knew. A tremor traveled slowly up her body and she reached up and ran her fingers through his dark curls, gripping his hair tightly as their kiss became more rampant. He lifted her onto his lap, and she straddled him, her wet pussy pressing against his straining cock, hindered only by the few inches of cotton between them. He devoured her mouth as though he would eat her alive, and she shook as the sensations racked her body. Her hot pussy pushed into his stony cock, and she felt him twitch excitedly.

It was too much.

The movement of his dick caused a tidal wave to surge through her heated body, and the position of it hit just the right spot to send her spiraling into an almighty orgasm. She screamed into his mouth, and he held her tighter as her hand gripped the back of his shoulder. She clung to him for dear life as an exquisite sensation exploded within her, leaving her gasping for air. As the wave washed over her, she stilled and snuggled into his ripped chest. His heart was thundering through him, and she smiled inside as she acknowledged he had not gone unaffected, either. She had never felt anything like this before in her life and was surprised to find herself sobbing hard into his embrace. He held her gently as a myriad emotions swept through her. She had no idea why she was crying, but she just let go.

"All right, darlin'?" Travis murmured as he nuzzled her soft hair.

Brooke was surprised at how calm she felt after her weep and nodded as she kissed his chest and snuggled into him.

After a few minutes, he moved her head so she faced him. She felt a little embarrassed at the thought of her tearstained face and knew her eyes would be puffy and red. He smiled at her tenderly.

"How long has it been?" he whispered gently.

She felt herself blush. "I used a vibrator the best part of a year ago when things really started to go wrong with Chad. It wasn't this good, though," she whispered, the care in his expression empowering her to answer.

He sighed. A flash of anger crossed his face, and then it was quickly replaced by a smile. He leaned forward and kissed her on the forehead before snuggling her in his strong arms again.

"Dinner will be served in one minute," Kent announced, popping his head around the door.

Brooke sat up straight, mortified that Kent should see her straddling Travis. For a brief second she thought it might cause trouble, but Travis's chuckle reminded her that these guys were into sharing in a big way. "I'll go get cleaned up," she muttered as she jumped from his warm lap.

Dinner was delicious. Kent Freeman sure was a fine cook! They chatted about their plans for the next few days and longer-term proposals for the ranch. Brooke was surprised to hear that Fred Hammond was planning to semi-retire within the next few months and Travis was going to take over some of his more advanced riding students.

"I'd be glad for some help once you're up to it." Travis grinned as he apparently read her mind. Brooke beamed up at him. It felt as though all her dreams were coming true.

"How are you with paperwork, Brooke?" Kent asked with a smirk.

"I did some work in the finance office at Robertson's Rubber," she replied eagerly, "and I'm good at admin."

"Well now. By the state of Travis's desk through there, I'd say he could do with a whole heap of help with that." Kent grinned.

"You might have a point there, buddy." Travis

nodded with a grimace. "I don't have a lot of time for all that pen-pushing stuff—much to the taxman's annoyance."

Brooke giggled. "I'd be more than happy to take a look."

The phone rang as they were finishing up their meal and Travis went over to answer it. "Don't you move," he warned Brooke, seeing her go to stand up and help clear the dishes. He was using that deep voice again, and she blushed as memories of earlier flashed through her mind and a gush escaped her pussy. *Damn!*

Brooke stayed put but couldn't resist stacking up the plates and cups ready for Kent to take to the sink. The deputy grinned at her as Travis chatted on the phone. They were going to have a hard time pinning her down for too long!

Chapter Seventeen

"How about a movie?" Travis suggested when he finished his conversation.

"Great." Brooke was delighted. The last time she'd watched TV was when she had her first night here with the guys, and she had loved it. The house was so warm and comforting, and the massive sofa accommodated all three of them perfectly, enabling them all to stretch out and enjoy the large screen that dominated the living room.

"There's some DVDs in the cabinet next to the TV, why don't you go choose one?" Kent suggested to her.

Brooke was grateful for a little freedom and slowly limped into the front room to check out the boys' collection.

~

Kent looked questioningly at Travis, who held back with him in the kitchen.

"Sheriff's having some trouble tracing any background on one of the builders," Travis told him with a frown.

"Which one?"

"A guy by the name of Kennedy. Says he's been traveling around looking for work for some time but hasn't had a lot of luck. He reckons that's why he's got no references or anything."

Kent frowned. "I don't know him. What's he like?"

"Quiet. Gets on with the job. No trouble to anyone. I might have a word with Hal, see if he can get anything out of him." Travis pouted.

"Good idea." Kent nodded. "Let's see how that goes. Folks often got their reasons for not broadcasting their business, and there's no reason to go about extracting this guy's life story without good reason. I nearly lost our girl trying that tack, after all."

Travis put a hand on Kent's shoulder and smiled. Kent smiled back and leaned in to give him a chaste kiss on the cheek. They made their way into the lounge to find Brooke sitting on the floor surrounded by DVDs.

"I can't decide," she explained, looking up at their grinning faces. They both chuckled and sat on the floor next to her. "You don't have any chick flicks, so I guessed you'd prefer an action movie or something. I don't want a war movie, so how about a Western or one of these thrillers?" She held up a couple of discs to them hopefully.

"You're supposed to be choosing something *you'd* like to see, baby. Never mind about us, we'll watch anything. Didn't we have some comedies in here some-where?" Kent got up and went back to the cabinet.

"Well, there were a few, but I figured you'd want something a bit more exciting." Brooke looked up at him in surprise.

"We'll get all the excitement we want later, darlin'. For now let's just enjoy a movie, shall we?" Travis murmured in her ear as he scooped up some of the discs.

Brooke flushed and her pussy clenched yet again. She stared at the floor and busied herself stacking up the DVDs with her good hand.

"How about one of these?" Kent handed her a pile of stand-up shows and a few comedy films. Brooke immedi-ately pounced on one of the films. "I've always wanted to see this!"

Travis took it from her and looked as though it was taking everything he had not to roll his eyes. Must be one of Kent's DVDs, Brooke thought. He passed the rest of their collection up to his lover and slid the disc into the player before helping Brooke up onto the massive sofa. As usual she sat between them—her favorite place. Kent dimmed the lights before settling down with them to watch the film, which had them all giggling and rolling about with laughter.

"Time for bed," Kent announced as the credits rolled, and he slid out from beneath Brooke to turn off the TV.

Brooke suddenly felt very nervous. She wasn't sure what the sleeping arrangements were yet. Last time she had been here she had stayed in one of the guest rooms, but really didn't want that now. She swallowed hard as Travis helped her to her feet. His hard cock press against her as she stood upright and looked up into his dark eyes.

"You're with us tonight," he told her with a wink.

Another gush escaped her pussy and she blushed. Travis chuckled. "Come on."

He showed her into the massive bedroom and she gaped. The bed was huge. More than adequate for the three of them. There were several wardrobes along one long wall, three double and three single. A massive mirror stretched across the top of three wide chests of drawers against another wall, and three comfy chairs surrounded a small round table in front of the picture window. Brooke noticed that on top of the chests of drawers, which doubled as a dresser, stood a range of toiletries. Giorgio Armani products sat on the left while Diesel were on the right. The space in the middle was clear, ready for her own choice of scent.

"We knew you'd come to us one day," Travis murmured seductively into her ear.

Brooke gazed up at his smiling face and flushed. It

was as though this was all preordained. No wonder she felt so at home here. She sighed happily.

"Your wash things are through there." Travis pointed to the en-suite bathroom, which, thankfully, had a proper door separating it from the main bedroom. "Kent and I tend to use the large bathroom at the end of the hall."

Brooke walked slowly over and opened the door to the small room. It was tastefully decorated in green, coordinating beautifully with the eau de nil of the main bedroom. It had a shower, hand basin, and toilet. She guessed that the dainty room wouldn't afford much room for her two capacious guys to wash their muscular bodies and smiled gratefully at the thought of her having her own private place for her most intimate activities.

As she prepared herself for bed, she heard Kent come into the bedroom. "All locked up," he announced.

"Thanks, Deputy." She could hear the grin in Travis's voice as he left the room, and she smiled.

Brooke left the bathroom wrapped in a towel. Kent was already lying on one side of the bed, his bare chest glowing in the light of the candles on either nightstand.

"I don't seem to have a nightgown," she explained. "Do you think I could borrow something of yours?"

Kent gazed at her. "Nope."

She gasped in surprise.

"You're ours now, darlin'." Travis growled as he entered the room in nothing but his Levis.

Brooke's heart pounded as she slowly walked toward the bed, trying to avert her eyes as he slid down his jeans to reveal his ripped naked body. As she crawled across the bed, Kent caught hold of her towel and she shrieked as her last piece of security was stolen from her. Travis scooped her up and laid her between them in the bed, drinking in her beauty before allowing her the luxury of covering herself with the soft duvet.

"How are you feeling?" Kent asked, cradling her head in his hands.

"I'm fine," she promised. She wasn't lying. Since coming home, she felt so relaxed and happy she had almost forgotten the pain she had been in so recently. The meds obviously helped a lot, but she was surprised at how normal she felt already. Her only hindrance was the cast, which held her arm in what felt like a ton of plaster, but she was getting used to doing everything one-handed.

"Brooke, baby, there's something you should know about us," Kent told her in a serious voice.

Her stomach lurched.

"We love you." Kent was staring into her eyes, and she felt a hot flame sear her body. She stared at him.

Travis's thumb slowly turned her face to his. His eyes were almost black and his face was shining. "What he said."

Brooke felt that she could float on air. "I love you both too," she admitted, gazing from one handsome face to the other.

Their solemn expressions were replaced by big cheesy grins, and they whooped and hollered as they wrapped their arms around her. She felt as though all her dreams were finally coming true and she just couldn't believe it.

The sharp jab in her butt made her jolt in surprise, and she reveled in the feel of Travis's bare cock nudging her into action. Her body was twisted slightly so she could face him as well as Kent; they were both so gorgeous she couldn't take her eyes off their faces. Her hand was resting on Kent's clean-shaven chest for support, as the boys' hands explored her skin gently. Travis's calloused fingers stroked up and down her back and shoulders, tickling the back of her neck and gliding down to her soft butt. He traced her scars tenderly before leaning down to kiss them, one by one.

Kent's soft hands caressed her hair, her face, and down her hips and over her soft stomach. He teased around the outside of her breasts and her inner thighs, making her squirm in anticipation. His lips sought hers and their tongues coasted lovingly to a dance of their own choreography.

Brooke drifted like a leaf on a summer breeze as sensations assuaged her battered body and mind. Her breathing slowly began to heave as the smoldering flame inside her once again burst to a flaming torch and she willed their hands to follow through with their promises. Her hips bucked against Kent's hand as he stroked her stomach, urging him to continue his caress down to her aching pussy. Her back arched as she tried to force her butt into Travis's hand and willed his licks and kisses to follow suit. She felt her nipples tighten and she pressed them into Kent's hot chest, and her tongue sucked on his as her need escalated. She could feel her pulsating pussy become wetter and pressed it into Kent's hip, desperate for some kind of purchase.

The throaty chuckles from her guys confirmed that they understood her demands and it didn't take them long to act on them. Travis was the first to slide his hand around to her dripping pussy, gliding though the swollen folds of her labia and skimming around her engorged clit. All the time he was nuzzling the back of her neck, murmuring to her how beautiful she was and what a gorgeous body she had. Kent's kisses became more urgent and his hands grazed over her breasts, gently puckering her hard nipples as she gasped into his hot mouth. Her arm grasped his shoulder and she clung on tight as waves of passion washed through her whole body, and her mind turned to delirious mush.

"She's so ready for us, bud," she heard Travis murmur as shivers racked her body. His fingers fondled her petals, and one ventured into her soaking pussy. Another joined it, and she gasped again as he began to finger-fuck her swollen cunt. His rock-hard dick was nudging at her ass, prodding the soft cushions of her butt. Kent unlocked her mouth as his kisses trailed down to her breast, where he sucked and pulled at her fleshy mounds. Brooke's hand grasped his fair hair as she yelped and nibbled at his fragrant neck. Moans filled the dimly-lit room as all three explored and caressed each other, their breathing becoming more rampant as their passion engulfed them.

"I want you, darlin'," Travis whispered in her ear as he grazed his finger around her clit, not quite touching the ultrasensitive tip.

"Yes, I want *you*," Brooke gasped desperately. She became aware of Kent stroking his thick cock as he slid up the bed. She licked her lips in response to the massive chunk of flesh, which wept its welcome to her. She dragged her eyes off his member to look into Kent's massive deep green eyes, which appeared hooded by his ardor. He was gazing lovingly at her.

"I want you too," she whispered breathlessly as he towered over her. Kent nodded and straddled her shoulders, pointing his meaty dick toward her welcoming mouth. Her tongue poked out and licked the pre-cum that glistened on the tip. It tasted almost sweet and felt like cream on her tongue. She laved his huge purple cockhead with her saliva, digging the tip of her hot tongue into the little groove on the underside, and exploring the collar which joined the bulbous head to the heaving shaft. She heard him gasp as he fed it slowly into her mouth, and she sucked and licked feverishly, digging the nails of her one good hand into his taut hip.

Kent hissed in delight, keeping his weight on his

knees. Brooke wondered if his cock ever had this much attention from a woman, because he truly seemed to be reveling in the moment.

Travis watched them for a few glorious minutes, still fondling her soft folds while stroking his own enormous dick. He spun around and knelt on the bed, stretching her legs wide enough to allow his ample body between them.

Brooke squealed as she felt Travis's tongue lavish her dripping pussy before his whole mouth surrounded it with wet heat. She felt herself clench and gasped around Kent's thick cock.

Travis chuckled before sitting back up and allowing his hot dick to probe her folds. Pre-cum added to the lubrication of her soaking pussy and he slid on a sheath before gliding easily into position, nudging her hard muscle in a quest for permission.

Brooke's loud groan was answer enough for him, and he gently pushed into her burning canal.

Brooke gasped, thrusting her head forward to consume more of Kent's cock, allowing the head to tickle the back of her throat as she opened it up for him. The sensations running through her body were inexplicable, but the fire that raged through her was tangible.

Travis pumped in a steady rhythm in and out of her soaking passage, and she almost screamed blue murder when he hit that spot she didn't even know she had. The sensation was exquisite, and she thrust her hips up, begging for more. She heard his low chuckle again, and he happily obliged, thrusting in and out in long, even strokes, while he caressed her hips and pubis with his huge, rough hands.

At the same time, Travis nuzzled into Kent's ripped back, licking and nipping his way around his neck and ears. The cowboy's taut chest rubbed against the deputy's back, eliciting groans from both of them.

She saw Kent gazing at her adoringly and her heart melted. Her hair was splayed out on the soft pillow, and she could feel her curls on her shoulders. He seemed so aroused by the sight of her sucking on his cock that she thought he was about to come there and then. Her big blue eyes were staring up at him, pleading with him. Her former pale skin was now covered in a warm pink flush, almost concealing the cuts and bruises that marred her skin.

Travis suddenly sped up his thrusts and with the cushion of his massive thumb brushed over the top of Brooke's hypersensitive clit. She screamed around the huge cock in her mouth as her orgasm swept through and her hips bucked uncontrollably under him. Kent grunted as his thick cum gushed down her open throat. Travis gave a loud groan as he came, pelting his seed toward Brooke's welcoming womb.

All three panted and shivered with aftershocks, holding on to each other for dear life. Kent withdrew from Brooke's mouth to allow her room to breathe, and he leaned back into Travis's ripped chest while stroking

Brooke's cheeks with his soft hands. Travis leaned forward onto his lover, reaching one hand around to stroke his soft chest while stretching the other down to caress Brooke's arm.

Eventually Kent moved away from Brooke's head and straightened out his cramped legs. Travis slowly withdraw his still-hard cock from her dripping pussy, and they both snuggled against either side of her, smiling but not speaking as satiation engulfed them. Each of the men had an arm around Brooke while linking their fingers together over her hand in the cast. Brooke's head was on Travis's panting chest while her free arm was draped over Kent's thundering heart. When they finally got their breath back, the boys leaned over their girl and kissed each other for a few long moments. Their eyes shone as they gazed at each other, and their skin glowed. Brooke had never seen them so happy and fulfilled. They bent down to kiss her reverently, inhaling her scent into their souls.

All of them had the most peaceful, content sleep of their lives. All their dreams had just come true.

Kent had already showered and put on his uniform when Brooke woke in Travis's arms the next morning. She lifted her head and watched in dismay as he combed his fair hair and slapped on his Diesel. A chuckle next to her made her look down at Travis's gorgeous smile, and she couldn't help but smile back.

"Some of us have a job to do, baby." Kent walked back over to bed and bent down to kiss her. His heavenly scent surrounded her, and she reached her arm up around his broad shoulder to welcome his tongue into her mouth.

"You eaten yet, buddy?" Travis asked as Kent stood up again.

"Yeah, I just had breakfast." Kent grinned, giving Brooke a sexy wink. She flushed. Travis rolled his eyes as he went to get out of bed.

"Don't you worry about me. Mason and I are having a breakfast meeting at the diner in an hour. I just want to get into the office and check on a few things first." Kent turned to his naked boyfriend, and they enjoyed a passionate embrace as they kissed good-bye.

"I'll try and pop back a bit later, see how you're all doing," Kent promised as he headed for the door.

Brooke sighed. She hadn't seen Kent in his uniform before, and the sight had an unholy effect on her.

"I'm going for a quick shower. You need to stay there and rest. You can get up later," Travis told her in that deep voice that made her flush. He grinned at her as his gorgeous, naked body slid out of the door and went down the hall.

Brooke snuggled back under the covers, breathing in the scents of both her men contentedly before falling back into a deep sleep. Her dream started sensually with both her men kissing her and touching her. She felt warm and deliriously happy in their arms. Then she became aware of a presence that frightened her. In a flash her men were gone and Chad West was standing there with a single tail whip in his hand, laughing cruelly. Brooke screamed and shot up in the bed.

Large hands held her and a firm voice was talking to her over and over. Through the sound of her own screams she could just make out the words.

"Open your eyes, Brooke. You're safe now. Open your eyes." The voice was commanding and authoritative; she had no choice but to obey it.

When she did, she stared straight into two large, brown eyes. Travis held her firmly by the shoulders and was talking to her constantly. That was the sound that had permeated her panicked brain. Her screams gradually stopped as she became aware of him, but the tremors were uncontrollable.

Once he was sure she had recognized him, Travis enveloped her in his strong, safe arms and murmured to her as she slowly came back to her senses.

At his command, she took deep breaths, inhaling him, allowing him to exorcise the demons that violated her thoughts. Her tears mingled with the water dripping from his body as she snuggled into his slightly hairy chest. Eventually he lifted her face up to look at him.

"It's all right, darlin'. You're safe now, d'ya hear?" His beautiful big eyes were as calm as his voice, and his whole face held a serenity she could cling to. She nodded. She was safe. She knew she was. Travis was here. Nothing could hurt her.

He kissed her forehead and stroked her shoulders. Brooke felt her heart slow down a beat with every touch he bestowed on her, and she reveled in his security and love.

Chapter Eighteen

The next few days passed slowly but happily for Brooke. Travis insisted she wasn't allowed out of the house, and when he had to go out to help the hands, he would arrange for Kent to pop back to sit with her for a while, or get Hal to babysit. At first she didn't mind as she was quite sleepy with all the drugs she was on.

After she had been home for about a week, and was able to walk without a limp, she was allowed to start doing some small jobs around the place. Travis showed her where everything was in the kitchen, and she was allowed to help him cook dinner for when Kent came home. She also spent long hours sorting through Travis's paperwork, which really needed some serious attention. His tax returns were in a mess and he was badly behind with his correspondence. She would have to wait another few weeks before the cast would be removed from her arm, enabling her to type, so she spent a lot of time using the computer with just one hand.

She and Travis were wading through a pile of receipts one morning when Hal's voice came over the radio. Travis quickly picked it up, always grateful for a distraction from paperwork.

"Are you OK for a few minutes while I pop out and give Hal a hand?" he asked Brooke with a frown. "Someone's managed to leave one of the gates open and a couple of the horses have disappeared. One of them's Mustard. He can be a bit of a handful when he's agitated."

"Of course," she said without looking up from the papers she was studying.

"Are you sure? I can see if Kent's free, though I know he said something about court this morning."

She smiled up at him, nodding. Her blonde curls fell about her shoulders, glistening like gold in the morning sun. "I'm fine, honestly. I shan't move from this chair if it makes you any happier."

"It does," he assured her as he planted a kiss on top of her head. "I won't be long."

Brooke resumed sorting out the papers. She guessed she had probably been part of the cause of the disarray—Travis had been too worried about her to worry about his tax returns—but she was determined to put it all straight. She was immersed in a heap of figures when she heard a noise outside the room.

"Did you manage to get him?" she called out, assuming Travis had returned.

The door opened and she looked up, smiling. Her blood ran cold and the air eluded her lungs as she stared right into a familiar face.

"Kenny? W-what are you doing here?" Her voice came out in a strangled squeal, and she stood up to face her enemy.

He sniggered derisively. "I work here, didn't you know? One of your dear lover boys pays me to hang around the ranch watching you. I've been waiting for the opportunity to pop in and say hello for some time now. I thought I'd never get him to leave you alone!" He moved toward her as he spoke.

"Y-you mean you...?" she stammered.

He nodded smarmily and reached out to her. Putting her broken arm under the lip of the desk for added weight, she used the other hand to tip the large table over toward him. He leapt back and she made for the door, screaming for help. He caught her and swung her around just as she got into the hallway and dragged her toward the boys' playroom.

"I wonder what we'll find in here." He gave an evil laugh as she pulled back. "I believe your other lover boy is a dab hand with a single tail, isn't he? Well let's just see how good I am with one, shall we?"

Brooke screamed again, doing her best to kick him while he held her firm by her good arm.

Kenny cursed as he tried the handle of the room only

to find it locked. "Where's the fucking key?" He demanded. "What have you done with it, you whore?"

Brooke stared at the closed door in astonishment. Why on earth would it be kept locked? "I don't know, I didn't know it was—"

He slapped her hard across her injured cheek, sending her tumbling to the floor in a heap as blood splattered up the wall.

Brooke felt stunned for a second, and then anger started to well inside her. She wasn't about to let this creep ruin everything for her. She had been a victim for long enough.

"Get your stinking hands off me, you bastard," she spat at him as he grabbed her good arm and hauled her to her feet.

He looked genuinely shocked for a fraction of a second, so she took the opportunity to shock him even more. "How dare you come into my home and threaten me, you scum? My men will kill you when they find you here, just like they did to Chad fucking West! Filth like you shouldn't be allowed to walk God's earth, and they'll make damn sure you don't!"

Kenny sneered angrily at her as he kicked the play-room door. "Your *gay* lover boys? You do realize they only let you stay here to make themselves look good, don't you? Everyone knows they'd rather be left alone to fuck each other to death. They'll soon get fed up with you, and once they've used you enough, they'll dump you like a hot potato!"

Brooke saw red. There was a time when she would have believed every foul word that crawled out of his rancid mouth, but not now. She was loved and she knew it.

"Bullshit! Travis and Kent love me and I love them. Nothing you can do or say will ever change that! We're for keeps. The three of us will be together forever and there's not a damn thing you or anyone else can do about it! Don't you *dare* violate our house with your filthy accusations and lies! You are the scum of the earth, do you know that? You're not worthy to lick their boots!" She yelled at him at the top of her voice, ignoring the thumps he was giving her.

"Do you know what you cost me, *whore*? Have you any idea how mad Chad was with me when you didn't sign that damn contract? Mad enough to refuse to pay me a fucking dime for my trouble! Now that your freaking nancy boys have killed him, I've got no way of ever making decent cash again, and it's all 'cause of you, bitch! You've ruined everything for me, d'you know that? Well guess what, I'm gonna make damn sure your cozy little arrangement here is ruined too, do you get that?" He slammed her into the locked door of the playroom, and she shrieked as pain wracked her good shoulder. As her pain turned to indignant rage, she kicked out at him, aiming for his puny balls. Not a very large target unfortunately, but her aim was adequate.

"You can't ruin anything for me, you scumbag! We love each other and no one in this whole world can change that!" she yelled at him as she kicked hard upward, trying to send his balls back to where they came from.

He howled and doubled over, releasing her as he grabbed something far more precious to him—his rapidly swelling scrotum.

She went to step over him to make her escape, but the bastard caught her ankle with one bony hand and twisted it until she screamed.

"Well said, darlin'. Now let go of her, you asshole, 'cause my finger's getting a little itchy here."

Brooke stared down the hallway where Travis stood pointing a rifle in their direction. Hal stood behind him with a shit-ass grin on his face and a revolver in his hand, also pointed at the bastard. Her heart, which was pumping ten to the dozen, now hammered for a totally different reason. Travis looked gorgeous! She managed to wriggle free of the fuckwad and ran over to them just as sirens wailed outside. Mason and Kent ran in, guns at the ready.

"Aw dammit. I was just getting into that!" Travis moaned as they took over the situation, cuffing the asshole and helping him as he staggered to the car. He handed his firearm over to Kent and swung a warm arm around Brooke's shoulder. She winced.

"Looks like we better get Doc Hardy back out here," Travis drawled with a frown as he gently cuddled their girl.

Brooke snuggled into his comfort as tears of relief

began to trail down her cheeks. He held her tighter, leading her into the lounge to sit down. She was shaking uncontrollably, and her sobs became stronger as she relaxed.

Hal slipped back to work as Kent returned to the house, having secured the prisoner in the SUV. "Mason's given me the rest of the day off," he announced as he offered Brooke a glass of water.

Brooke was about to tell Kent he didn't need to take any more time off on her account when she caught his expression for the first time since he'd arrived. He looked pale with shock. Travis looked tense too, and she realized how scared they had been for her.

"I should never have allowed him onto the ranch without knowing his background," Travis moaned a short while later when they were all relaxing over lunch. "I was too set on getting the work started quickly."

"Well, it explains why we couldn't find anything on him." Mason sighed, having secured the prisoner in a cell and returned to see how they were all doing.

"His name's Kenny. He was a friend of Chad's," Brooke told them in a small voice.

A knock at the door made Brooke jump in Travis's arms. He soothed her with soft kisses to her head as Kent went to answer it. Doc Hardy and the counselor, Sarah Harris, arrived at the same time.

While the doctor checked out Brooke's injuries, Kent

took Sarah into the kitchen and filled her in on the morn-ing's events.

"Will she be OK?" Travis asked as the elderly doctor frowned at the wound on Brooke's face that had opened again slightly.

"Yeah. She'll be fine." He carefully cleaned her up and placed a fresh dressing over her cheek before exam-ining her shoulder. "This shoulder's going to bruise quite a bit. It's taken quite a knock but nothing's broken." He seemed satisfied by the time he picked up his battered old hat and headed out the door, muttering something about rest and painkillers.

Sarah Harris spent several hours chatting with Brooke that afternoon. They talked about everything from the recent events to their shared love of horses. By the time she left, Brooke was smiling brightly and feeling much better.

Brooke made her way into the kitchen where the boys were enjoying a sweet embrace while something tasty was cooking for dinner. She watched them for a few minutes, smiling. They seemed to take it in turns to be the most dominant in their relationship, and their love for each other was palpable.

Kent had changed out of his uniform and looked almost edible in his tight jeans and smart blue shirt. He had one hand inside Travis's partially unbuttoned plaid shirt, and Brooke knew he would be stroking the soft hairs that graced Travis's ripped chest. His other hand was on the cowboy's muscular shoulder. Travis had one hand around Kent's thick, taut waist, gripping his belt, while the other stroked his fair hair. They were enjoying a deep kiss, slurping and sucking at each other's tongues, while chuckles emanated from their throats.

Brooke loved seeing them together like this, so intimate. She turned to go, afraid she was intruding on their private moment, when Kent called out to her. "Come and join us, baby."

She gazed up at them. Their eyes were hooded, and they were obviously still in the moment as they smiled over to her. Kent held a hand out to her, which she wasted no time in taking. As she stood sandwiched between them, she could feel their warmth. She snuggled close to them both and they embraced her. They took turns to kiss her at first, and then all three were kissing each other as moans filled the air of the little kitchen.

Brooke smiled up at their handsome, shining faces when they finally loosened their grip.

"Did you have a good gossip with Sarah?" Travis teased.

"I had a very helpful counseling session, if that's what you mean," Brooke replied with mock indignation.

Kent chuckled. "That's you told, bro."

"Well, all I heard was talk about horses," Travis said with a pretend pout.

Brooke gasped. "You were listening in to our conversation?" She and Sarah had been given the privacy of the lounge while the boys sorted out the mess in the office. Apart from talking about the incidents both from this morning and the ongoing trauma with Chad West, Brooke had confided in Sarah about her feelings for the guys. After such a shaky start, she couldn't be happier with them both. She blushed a little, wondering just how much Travis had heard.

"Only for a second. This killjoy wouldn't let me hang around," Travis replied sulkily.

Kent chuckled again, stroking Travis's hair and gazing into his big brown eyes. "I told you, bro. Some things are just too private to be shared," he pretended to admonish him.

Brooke giggled. She could just imagine Kent having to pry Travis away from the door; he understood all about confidentiality. She snuggled into them, wishing she didn't have that dang cast on her arm so she could cuddle them both at once.

They enjoyed a delicious dinner, which the boys had proudly prepared between them. Brooke hadn't realized how late in the day it was. She must have been talking with Sarah for hours. Afterward, they refused to let her lift a finger while they cleared up the dishes, sending her into the lounge to watch some TV for a while. In truth, the guys probably thought it a good way to take her mind off the harrowing events of the day.

"Do you want to watch a movie tonight?" Kent suggested as they joined her on the sofa a while later.

"No, I want to talk." She clicked off the TV as they took their usual places, one either side of her.

"OK," Kent said quietly, "shoot."

"Why was your playroom door locked?" she asked him warily.

Kent stared at her. He cleared his throat a little nervously. "We thought it best after what happened before when you saw me..."

"Practicing," she finished for him.

He nodded. "I didn't know anything about your past experience then. I didn't mean to scare you," he assured her.

"But don't you still need to keep practicing? I know you haven't been to the club since I've been living here, but surely..."

"We're not into that anymore," Travis interjected quietly.

Brooke spun around to face him her eyes wide. "You're not into BDSM?"

"Baby, we don't want to frighten you. We realize you've had some real bad experiences with BDSM, so we decided to drop the lifestyle. We want you to feel safe with us," Kent explained.

She stared back at him. "But it's part of you. It's your lifestyle. It's what you enjoy. And you're damn good at it! I saw you at Ty's. Kent, you were brilliant. You can't just give it up."

Kent smiled at her kindly. "Things have changed now. We want you to stay with us, forever. You can't stay if you don't feel safe."

"But I *do* feel safe with you. I know I overreacted. Stella explained to me that I'd got it all wrong. I wanted to learn about the lifestyle because there were elements of it I felt I needed—I *still* need. One of the things I love about you two is your natural dominance. I thought Chad was dominant, but now I realize he was just a bullying asshole. He hurt me because it made him happy to make me miserable. I know now that it shouldn't be like that. When I saw you at the club with your sub, I realized just how wrong I'd been about it all. You weren't hurting her; she was loving what you were doing and so were you. You can't throw that away." Her eyes pleaded with him as she held on to his arm.

Kent and Travis exchanged a look.

"You mean, you still want to learn about the lifestyle?" Kent asked her slowly while studying her face.

"Yes. I know you think I'm fragile, but I'm not really." Her eyes were as big as saucers as she stared up at his gorgeous face.

"I can vouch for that, buddy. You should have seen her kicking that asshole in the balls today. There was nothing fragile about that. And the language that came out of her potty mouth was enough to make your hair curl!" Travis chuckled.

A massive grin crossed Kent's handsome face. "You sure about this, baby? I mean, I promise neither of us will harm you in any way."

"Yes," she whispered. "I want you two to teach me. I trust you."

Kent took her in his massive arms and squeezed her tight. "OK. You've got it," he promised with a chuckle.

Brooke sank into the warmth and safety of her hero and held him for what seemed like forever. When he finally released her, Travis spun her around and took her in his loving embrace. He kissed the top of her head, and she could almost feel him smiling as he held her.

"Can we start now?" She smiled eagerly at Travis.

"Now, hold on a minute. I think we'd better wait until you're fully recovered first." Kent told her.

She pouted, still looking at Travis. He grinned. "Well I suppose we could start with a few basic positions and stuff. And there's no harm in showing her around the playroom, just to get acquainted with it," Travis relented.

Kent sighed. "OK. But none of the physical stuff yet, agreed?"

"*If* she's not up to it." Travis nodded with a wicked grin.

They led her down the hall as her stomach did somersaults, and Kent took the key from his pocket. He unlocked the door and opened it wide. They stood in the doorway for a few minutes, allowing Brooke to take in the sight before her. Last time she had only been aware of Kent throwing a single tail. Nothing else had registered. Now she gazed in amazement. A St. Andrew's Cross was attached to one wall, with several rings and fastening hanging from it. A spanking bench stood to one side, and a hammock-style sling hung across the other side of the room. A tall dresser stood near the door, while above it were racks holding an assortment of whips, paddles, and floggers.

She took a deep breath, and then ventured into the dimly lit room. It was warm and surprisingly calming. Travis and Kent stood back while she inspected the apparatus, running a hand across the smooth spanking bench and reaching up to test the height of the large cross. She noticed the single tail whip that hung over the dresser and her breath hitched. Swallowing hard, she went over to it, studying it and the other implements hanging there.

Her hands trembled as she touched the drawer knobs, and Kent nodded his assent. She pulled open one of the heavy drawers to find a violet wand complete with various attachments, and some beautiful bejeweled nipple clamps. Another drawer held gags, including ball gags and blindfolds of varying colors and shapes, as well as a selection of cuffs and hogties. An assortment of smaller floggers and paddles filled another drawer, while the bottom one held a couple of spreader bars. There were a couple of smaller drawers toward the top of the dresser that she didn't look into.

Brooke turned to Travis, who was still leaning in the doorway. He cocked a sexy eyebrow at her, and she felt a hot burn inside her. Kent was standing next to her, studying her reactions, saying nothing.

She closed the last drawer and turned back to the spanking bench. It had soft leather upholstery and felt cool under her shaking fingers. She bit her lip, trying to envisage what it would feel like to be spanked over it. She looked questioningly at Kent, who had followed her over.

"I think she wants to check it out, buddy," Travis called over with a chuckle.

Kent sighed. "*Do* you, baby?" His beautiful face held a sexy inquiry, which mingled with a little concern and a whole lot of lust.

Brooke's breath hitched. She nodded slowly.

Chapter Nineteen

Having watched Brooke strip out of her jeans, top, and pretty satin underwear, Kent carefully tied her to the padded spanking bench. One arm was still in plaster, so she carefully laid it over her head while he secured her free hand and her ankles to the rings attached to the sides. Travis would keep a firm grip on her back throughout to ensure she couldn't slip. Kent could sense her excitement, and his own heart raced at the sight of her beautiful, soft body, laid out for them.

"What's your safe word, baby?" he asked as he removed his own shirt.

She was staring over her shoulder at him, wide eyed, when he threw his shirt to one side and hovered over her expectantly.

"You do *have* a safe word, don't you?"

She shook her head. "Chad said I didn't need one."

He felt his whole body tense momentarily, and he took a deep breath to quell his anger.

"Fuckwad!" Travis was standing at the other side of her, also shirtless.

"You *always* need a safe word, baby. We'll use the traffic light system. Red for stop, yellow to slow down or pause, and green for go. Understood?" Kent's voice was firm but calm, a testament to his self-control.

Brooke nodded. She breathed in the beauty of her two handsome hunks. Their presence was calming, and she settled peacefully onto the bench, her head turned to face Kent.

"The spanking we're going to give you today is purely for pleasure. This is *not* a punishment, do you understand?" Kent asked gently.

"Yes, Sir," she whispered as she sank deeper into the cool bench. Her eyes opened wide as what she'd said sunk in.

Kent was smiling at her. "I like that." He nodded with a grin. "You will call us both 'Sir' when we're topping you, understand?"

Brooke grinned, hearing Travis chuckle behind her. "Yes, *Sirs*," she replied.

"Good. Now, some of these welts still look a little raw, so we'll be doing our best to avoid them. Don't hesitate to use your safe word if it starts to hurt, though, OK?"

Brooke nodded.

Kent was the first to strike her butt. His hand felt like

a blunt thud on her skin. She sighed as it ricocheted through her body. Travis was next. Again, not a sting, just a satisfying thud. The boys took turns. Their intensity grew, but there was still no pain. The thud began at the base of her butt, and heat seemed to travel up it.

"You OK, darlin'?" Travis's voice was tender, and she wished she could see his gorgeous face, but she couldn't bring herself to move her head.

"Yes, Sir," she told him with a smile.

As they continued to smack her behind, the sensations became more intense. Her hands and feet were tied at either side of the bench, leaving her pussy gaping across the top of the now-warm leather. She gasped as she realized her juices were running down the side of the bench. She was becoming more aroused than she ever thought possible, though she had never experienced anything remotely like this before.

The boys murmured to her all the time about how beautiful she was and how much they loved her body, and she melted into the bench. Her eyes were closed, and she was surrounded by the sounds, scents, and the mere presence of the two men she loved more than life itself.

"You enjoying this, baby?" Kent didn't really need to ask. The smile on her face and the evidence dripping down the bench and forming a small puddle on the floor told him everything he needed to know.

"Yes, Sir," she whispered without opening her eyes. She was floating on a cloud of ecstasy and never wanted to come down.

Her eyes did pop open, though, when Travis's fingers slid into her pussy. "Oh yeah. She's enjoying it, all right." She could hear his self-satisfied grin.

He gently stroked her clit, and she squealed as shock and delicious sensations shot through her languid body. Her pussy clenched, and it thrummed as she slowly recovered.

"Do you want me, baby?" Kent's hot breath seared across her ear, and she thought she would come on the spot.

"Yes, oh God, yes!"

She was trembling, and her whole body was burning hot inside and out. Travis was running his finger through her labia and trailing the juices up to her small, tight rosette. His finger pressed on it gently, and she gasped at the sensation.

"I'm going to have that pretty pink ass of yours later," he promised her as he came to stand in her line of vision.

A flame seared through her body at the thought of it, and she stared up at his gorgeous face. As Travis unfastened her hand, Kent took his position behind her, heeling off his boots and kicking off his Levis. He gripped her hips, keeping her firmly in position.

She felt his thick cock nudging at the mouth of her sopping-wet pussy, and he glided into her. He stilled for a moment, allowing her to become accustomed to his heaving girth before he thrust hard and long, causing her to moan deliciously.

Travis had unzipped his fly and allowed his huge member to spring free. His cockhead gave her a wet kiss as he neared her lips, and she licked at his juices eagerly before devouring his massive cock in her hot mouth. Travis's cock tasted quite salty as she slurped and sucked at it. She swiped her tongue up and down its lengthy shaft, staring up at his lustful face. His eyes were hooded and he clenched his teeth, trying to maintain control of his body.

With her free hand, Brooke pumped at his column, sucking hard at the delicious pre-cum that dripped into her welcoming mouth. She heard Travis gasp as she grabbed his hip for support, taking every inch of his swollen cock into her burning mouth and down her gaping throat. Luckily she had no gagging reflex and was able to take either of her men just as they liked it, much to their untold delight.

She could feel Kent gouging a hot trail through to her womb, his heaving thrusts conveying his mounting passion as she pushed back against him. He released one of his hands to tickle her clit as his vast member grazed deliciously over her sensitive G-spot. Sensations soared with every movement he made. Her nerve endings jangled as he pulled back and then thrust forward until his balls slapped noisily against her.

The room smelled of sex, sweat, and their individual scents, while the sounds of slurping, moans, and flesh-on-flesh filled the air. Their grunts and shrieks became louder, the mere sound a delectable aphrodisiac to one another.

The fire ripped through Brooke's body and she screamed around Travis's huge cock. The vibrations at the back of her throat were enough to unhinge him, and he yelled as he came in massive bursts, flooding her with his cream. Brooke didn't waste a drop of his burning nectar and swallowed greedily as it flowed down her open throat.

Kent couldn't hold on any longer and let go with a deep guttural grunt as his seed swamped her enticing womb. He thrust over and over as the deluge emptied from his enormous cock.

Travis removed his dick as Brooke panted for air, and he held her firm while Kent quickly untied her ankles. He swept her up in his bulging arms and carried her effortlessly to their bedroom. Kent followed, still gasping for air.

They lay, breathing heavily as they recovered in the comfort of the soft bed. Brooke had her head on Kent's soft chest while her arm was draped over her cowboy. After a while, Travis stood and removed his jeans.

Brooke opened her lazy eyes and saw him outlined in the moonlight that now streamed through the open window. His muscles were highlighted in the silvery glow, and his eyes twinkled in the dim light. A shadow crossed his ripped chest, but even the darkness couldn't hide the massive erection that grazed his stomach. His muscular legs took a step nearer to the bed, and she noticed, with horror, that he had caught her staring at him. His eyebrow hitched questioningly, and she flushed with embarrassment. He chuckled.

"See anything you like, darlin'?"

Brooke gasped.

A hand stroked her back, and she realized Kent had been watching them. "It's all right, baby. He has a gorgeous body. There's no harm in admiring it. I do it all the time." Kent's voice was quiet and reassuring.

She turned around to face him and noticed he was actually stroking his own massive cock. The sight of his two lovers had aroused him.

"You tired, darlin'?"

She felt the bed dip as Travis crawled back over toward her. Suddenly she was wide awake. She smiled up at him. Travis leaned over her, twisting her onto her back with her head still on Kent's ripped chest. The cowboy raised her good arm above her head, resting it on Kent's torso, where he held it while he grazed his lips over hers, lapping at her seam with his hot tongue.

"I love you," he whispered into her mouth as she allowed him entry, and their tongues twisted and danced in their heat.

Brooke didn't get chance to reply as her breath hitched, and she was aware that Travis's other hand was on Kent's huge dick. He caressed and stroked his lover while becoming more insistent with his tongue in her mouth. Kent groaned beneath her head as Travis pulled at his shaft and she could hear the splashing sound as the deputy's pre-cum lubricated his lover's fingers.

Kent trailed his hand down to her pussy, and he stroked the juices he found there all over her pubis. He probed her dripping canal with his large fingers, and wiped her wetness down across her. The sensations made her buck under his hand, and she moaned with delight. He continued to stroke her labia and spread her cream right around to her ass, causing her to automatically lift her hips to allow him entry. She felt him spread her natural lubricant around her tight rosette, and her breath hitched excitedly.

She felt Travis begin to thrust his tongue in and out of her mouth, as if fucking it, and she glowed with the heat of her passion. Her own tongue was languid as his slid over it time and again. His tongue was hard and tickled her lips before bursting into her hot mouth and hitting the back of her throat. She closed her eyes, imagining it was his cock again, and her breathing heaved noisily.

"Do you want us, darlin'?" Travis whispered into her mouth.

Brooke whimpered. "Yes!" Her eyes stared into his, pleading him to take her.

Travis lifted his weight off the bed and effortlessly placed Brooke straddling Kent's enormous dick. Kent took her weight and allowed her to lower herself slowly onto his heaving member. She gasped at the massive girth entering her, and stilled when she finally reached his rock-hard balls.

Kent pulled her head toward his and took her mouth in a sensual, lingering kiss. Her whole body relaxed on him, and he reached a hand down to stroke her breasts lovingly. Brooke moaned as the sensations flowed through her. Kent slowly lifted her, and she held his shoulder as he pushed her back down on his throbbing cock before slowly lifting her again. Brooke followed his pace and settled into steady rhythm as Travis took his position behind her.

"This ass ever been fucked before, darlin'?" Travis seemed to have his suspicions as his finger tantalized her pink rosette, but he obviously felt compelled to ask.

"Yes, but not..." Brooke stilled as a vision flashed in front of her mind. Chad had insisted and it hurt—*bad*. She felt her muscles tense, and her skin pricked all over.

"Shh." Kent's reassurance warmed her, and his sensual kisses began to wrap her in a warm glow again. Travis was stroking her back, and slowly her muscles began to relax again.

"You still have your safe word, darlin'," Travis whispered into her ear.

She felt every fiber in her body ease and she sucked softly at Kent's tongue.

"That's it, darlin', just relax," Travis soothed her as he lingered with his hand down her back and caressed her sensitive perineum. "Just remember we love you, honey, and we're gonna make this wonderful for you, I promise."

His voice was low and his pledge went straight to her pussy. She gushed and Travis immediately trailed his fingers through her juices and around to her ass.

Kent resumed lifting her up and down his thick shaft, and she sighed as she picked up the rhythm once again and the sensations flowed through her. He slowly upped the pace, and she gasped into his mouth. Her breath began to pant, and she screwed her eyes tight as tremors began to rack her body.

"Lean right over, baby." Travis used his Dom voice and she gushed violently again.

With his large finger he swirled her cream into her hole, followed by a great dollop of cold lube. She jumped at the sensations and then gasped as his finger delved down to the thick rim of tissue.

"Deep breaths now, darlin', breathe out slowly." Travis's competent voice was calming and reassuring as it seeped into her world, and she began to inhale.

As she exhaled, his finger carefully broke through her barrier and eased itself into her private domain. The pain she expected didn't come. There was a feeling of pressure but it didn't hurt. She opened her eyes in surprise, still breathing deeply.

"You're doing great, baby." Kent smiled at her, and she saw the slight strain in his gorgeous face. He thrust hard into her as Travis withdrew his finger. Brooke yelped. The sensations Travis caused by pulling back out were even better than when he entered her, and the force of Kent's hard dick had sent her nerve endings jangling.

"Right over now, darlin'," Travis urged as he rubbed another handful of lube over his pulsating cock. He waited for her to exhale again before nudging his dick up to her rim and then thrusting it into her as Kent withdrew.

"Aah!" Brooke was stunned at the millions of sparks lit through her entire body and she cried out. Travis grunted as he tunneled deep into her before slowly withdrawing almost all the way back.

She almost felt bereft at the loss of his throbbing member, but then Kent pounded her down hard onto his cock and she yelped again. The boys settled into a steady rhythm, like pistons chugging in and out of her oversensitized body, and Brooke lost herself in them. Kent continued to nibble at her lips as she yelped and gasped, and she could hear his rapid breathing as they kissed. His hands slid between them and massaged her breasts, one by one, before tugging and pinching at her hard nipples.

Travis slipped a hand down and stroked her clit while his other hand clamped to her hip. She could hear him grunting behind her and imagined his gorgeous face as he pumped into her.

Suddenly the whole world began to spin as the boys suddenly rocketed the pace and Travis pinched hard on her pulsating clit, sending her soaring into an almighty orgasm that caused her to emit an ear-splitting scream against Kent's ripped chest.

Kent let out a savage roar and shot his boiling seed straight to her womb while Travis gave a feral howl as he exploded, spurting his cum like molten lava searing through her passage. The room was electric as their elation peaked, and they all gasped and panted while whimpers and moans escaped their throats.

Brooke was quaking as she slumped heavily onto Kent's heaving chest and she felt Travis's weight on her back. Her eyes closed and she gulped in mouthfuls of air. She could hear her lovers huffing as they all gradually relaxed.

Travis rolled off her heated body, and she immediately felt a waft of cool night air flow across her back. She trembled at the sensation. He noticed her quivering and lifted her from her lover's body to wrap her in a cool sheet. Brooke's eyes were still closed, but she nodded her acknowledgment and curled up on the bed. Travis used the en suite to freshen up, keeping an eye on her through the bathroom mirror.

He returned to the bed and cuddled into their beautiful girl while Kent stirred. The deputy smiled at the other two cuddled up together and leaned over to give Travis a loving kiss before he went for a wash.

Their girl slowly came to her senses when the bed dipped and Kent returned to them. Her lips turned up in a smile. Brooke lazily leaned her head on Travis's heaving chest, while reaching her arm out to stroke Kent's torso.

Each of her men had an arm around her and, as usual, they linked their fingers over the hand in her cast. She sighed softly. For the first time in her life, she felt truly happy. Truly loved. Truly safe.

The End

Next in this series:

THE MEN OF MOONE MOUNTAIN
BOOK TWO

Here's an excerpt...

Red-Light Wrangler
MM Romance

Rich pulled up his pants and rummaged about for his shirt. He grinned at the blond-haired guy who lay slumped on the bed, panting for breath.

"That was great, friend," the cowboy said with a nod as he dragged on his boots. "Friend" was much easier than trying to remember the name of everyone he fucked.

"Will I see you again?" The blond guy sat up slowly. The candlelight glowed over his ripped body, outlining his muscles. Rich had been very taken with the guy's body when he'd seen him in the bar, and found his face quite handsome to look at. However, once he'd brought Rich back to this shithole the cowboy's perception of him changed in a heartbeat. He'd stuck around for a fuck though—it was late and he was horny as hell.

"Never know your luck," Rich smirked as he threw a pile of notes on the nightstand.

"Hey, now, I'm not a…" the guy began, but couldn't hide the way his eyes widened when he saw the denomination of the cash.

"Never said you were. I just thought you might do me the courtesy of keeping your mouth shut about all this. I don't want folks knowing my business if you catch my drift?" Rich winked and left the crummy apartment.

It was dark, but he welcomed the cool breeze which whipped around him as he hurried over to his car. The night air was a lot fresher than the stench in that rank apartment.

The engine of his cobalt-blue Bugatti Veyron purred as he backed out of the tiny yard and swiftly made his way to the interstate. His rule of never crapping on his own doorstep sure was a bummer on nights like this when all he wanted was his own bed. He couldn't conceive staying in that place any longer than he had to though, and pitied the blond guy. He seemed real nice; it made him wonder how he'd ended up in a hellhole like that.

About a half hour later, he was driving through the deserted main street of Moone, with the majestic Moone

Mountain towering over it. At the foot of the mountain he veered off to the right and pulled into the long drive of the Buchanan Ranch. His was the cabin in the grounds not far from the entrance. Although "cabin" was probably an understatement as it was bigger than most folks' family homes.

As he got out of the car he glanced over at the massive ranch house. A light was on in the study window. Looked like Dad was burning the midnight oil again. The old man hardly seemed to sleep at all these days. He shrugged and let himself into his house, not bothering with the lights as he hauled his tired ass up the stairs to his bedroom. He wasn't too tired for a shower though. Afterward he flopped onto his freshly made queen-size bed and crashed out.

Rich was up at dawn when the bright orange sunlight streamed through his open window. He pulled on his plaid shirt and clean Levi's before heading to the kitchen for some much needed coffee.

He took his mug with him to the stable block where he met up with Lucas Hammond, the ranch foreman. Lucas was leading out a couple of grays and grinned when he saw him approach.

"Morning, sir, your dad's looking for you. Said something about you being ready for the wedding in a couple of hours."

"Dang! I clean forgot it was today. We've got a new guy, the assistant foreman, starting around mid-morning. I was hoping to show him 'round. Dad said he came with some good references, should be a boon to the ranch. I haven't got time for cavorting at Emma-Leigh's weddin' today!" Rich cursed as he slammed the stable door shut.

"Your dad seemed quite insistent on it," Lucas explained apologetically.

"Yeah, I'll bet he did. Emma-Leigh's the daughter he never had. He always envied Uncle Ted getting a boy *and* a girl." Rich sighed.

"Well, I can take the new guy around if you want? Show him the ropes? I need to get to know him anyhow as he'll be my assistant," Lucas offered.

Rich ran a hand through his tousled, dark waves in frustration. He had caught a glimpse of the new guy when his dad interviewed him and couldn't wait to meet him. From what he'd seen, the guy was HOT!

He was hopping mad that he hadn't been allowed to sit in on the hiring procedure, but his dad had insisted he was needed out on the ranch to deal with the whole missing horse situation. What a mess that'd been so far.

"All right. The guy's name is Nathan Walker and he's due in around ten," Rich relented. "I'll get away as soon as I can. If I don't catch him today, we'll have to meet up tomorrow. There's a few things I need to go through with him about the job."

Lucas frowned. "Everything OK, boss?"

"Sure." Rich nodded. "I'm gonna take Sparky out for a bit," he added and made his way over to his favorite horse's stall.

The sun was rising fast and the day was set to be a scorcher. They didn't have many really hot days here in the foothills of the mountain, but this summer they seemed to be enjoying quite a few. Rich tipped his hat back slightly to keep the heat from the back of his neck. He took a good look at the massive ranch which would one day be all his. He couldn't wait—not that he wished anything bad on his dad, of course. He just felt sometimes that the hands didn't respect him the way they should, and his dad didn't give him all the responsibility he wanted.

He was good at his job, he knew that. Heck he'd been doing it all his life. He was in the saddle before he could walk. His mother had seen to that. He'd ridden all his life and enjoyed working as a wrangler on the ranch as soon as he'd been old enough. He'd been proud of his job, and still regarded himself a wrangler even though nowadays he spent more time sitting at his computer. He supposed that's why he didn't seem to get that much respect from the hands. Some of the older guys in particular still regarded him as Rich the Wrangler instead of Mr. Buchanan, the boss's son.

Rich looked over to where a couple of the experienced hands were breaking in a young stud. His mom used to help with that. She had the patience of a saint, and everyone loved her. It had been fifteen years now since the cancer killed her.

Dad had become a different person after her death. He seldom laughed any more. He was real fond of his niece though, and had been looking forward to her wedding for months. Rich grinned. He daren't tell his dad he didn't really want to attend, and certainly couldn't tell him the reason why.

"I hope you're planning on making an effort today, son." Frank Buchanan's voice boomed from behind him, and he turned from where he was idly stroking Sparky to face him.

"Morning, Dad. Yeah, I was just on my way now to get showered and changed," he lied.

"Well, I hope so, son. Your Aunt and Uncle are relying on us for some support today. It's a big day for them—hell, for everyone! The only girl in the family. Your Aunt Millie's bound to be a bag of nerves, mother-of-the-bride and all that. Women get very emotional about these things." Frank's voice was gruff, but Rich detected a tear in the corner of his eye. It was a bigger day for him than he was letting on.

"Yes, sir, I'm on it," he promised his dad and strolled back to the cabin to get ready.

The wedding was an enormous affair, with what looked like the whole of Moone County and neighboring Reedlake County in attendance. It took place on the Meredith Ranch, which Uncle Ted and Aunt Millie owned, and was home to their twins, Emma-Leigh and Joey. A massive tent had been set up by the lake and the whole area was decked out in pink and white roses to match the bride's bouquet.

Rich smiled at everyone and made polite conversation until an acceptable time to find the bar. He downed a couple of rum and Cokes in quick succession, reveling in the burn in his throat. It had been quite a day and it wasn't over yet.

"Thought I'd find you here," Joey Buchanan sneered as he came up behind him, a glass of champagne in his hand. He looked very dapper in a navy suit and a light brown crew cut. He wasn't a bad-looking guy, but whenever Rich saw him he always grimaced which made him look quite ugly.

"Yep, I needed a *real* drink," Rich replied without looking up. He studied the glass in his hand.

"We were reserving those for the *real* men," Joey sniped.

Rich slammed the glass on the counter and stood up. "Just what in heck is that supposed to mean?" He felt his blood boil as he towered over his cousin. He had had just about enough of him already. The young guy had been scowling and frowning at him all day.

Joey squared up to him. "What do you think it means?" he demanded angrily.

The tent went quiet and people started staring their way.

"Don't you dare ruin your sister's wedding," Rich growled. He finished his drink in one gulp and smiled to the guests as he made his way toward the buffet.

"You OK, Aunt Millie?" He put an arm around the little round lady.

She had had a very emotional day, and was now smiling brightly at everyone. Her face shone up at him and her eyes twinkled.

"Oh, Rich, I'm so glad you came. I'm fine, my dear, just a bit teary-eyed back there for a bit. It's not every day your daughter gets married. Now when is it going to be your turn? You should have been first, being the eldest and all." She hooted with laughter and Rich grinned back at her. How many times had he heard this?

"Ha. That'll be the day," Joey sniped from behind them.

Rich's jaw tightened and his fists clenched.

"Now, Joey, don't be awful. Your cousin's a good-looking guy. I'm sure he could have any woman he wanted, couldn't you, dear?" She stroked Rich's cheek tenderly.

"Trouble is, he doesn't want a *woman*, do

you, *dear*?" Joey chided and pinched Rich's other cheek hard between his finger and thumb.

Rich seethed, but was determined not to make a scene.

Just then there was a clanging sound as the emcee hit a glass with the back of a spoon to signal the start of the speeches. There was a flurry of activity as people rushed to their seats, and Millie dragged her son with her. Being at the top table, Joey was facing into the room, glaring daggers at Rich. Rich remained standing and took a glass of champagne from a passing waiter, which he tipped pointedly to his cousin.

The speeches gave Rich a welcome opportunity to take a good look around at the guests. He knew most of them—heck, he was *related* to a good many—but there were a few new faces.

A handsome guy with sandy-colored hair and big green eyes caught his attention, and he made a mental note to catch up with him later. The guy looked his way and smiled. Rich nibbled at some more of the buffet until Uncle Ted's speech made him look up.

He had said all the usual stuff about how wonderful his daughter was and had now turned his attention to the ranch.

"I will be retiring in two years' time," he went on, "and I will be handing over the reins, so to speak." There was raucous laughter at this. "Anyway, the Meredith Ranch will be given to my children, half of it going to Joey and the other half to Emma-Leigh and Ryan. I need them to start taking over while I'm still around to keep an eye on things, so after the honeymoon I am going to start taking a backseat. I trust that Joey and Ryan will make a good job of running it and allowing me some peace and quiet in my old age." Again the audience laughed.

Rich looked over to see Joey fuming, and he grinned. He had always claimed that his dad would leave the ranch to *him*, as Emma-Leigh had shown no interest in managing it, but now that she was married to Ryan things were a little different. Ryan Randall practically ran the Meredith already, which until now hadn't been a problem to Joey. It allowed the boss's son to flounce around the estate with his nose in the air, giving out his orders to anyone he saw. Rich couldn't help sniggering at the look on the young guy's face.

Emma-Leigh jumped up and hugged her dad, and Ryan shook his hand happily. Joey didn't even try to smile when he stood to shake his father's hand, but Ted didn't seem to notice. The congregation were all clapping and cheering. It was a terrific start in life for the newly-weds. The more Joey seethed, the more Rich chuckled.

He soon became fed up of all the filthy looks he was receiving from his cousin, so Rich took another Bacardi and Coke from the bartender and headed outside. It was quieter out there, with just a few guests milling about.

He took a leisurely stroll down to the lake and sat on the grass to enjoy the peace and the warm sun. He chuckled as he thought how pissed Joey looked that he was having to share his inheritance. It was a well-known fact that the Meredith Ranch wasn't doing as well as the Buchanan, and Rich knew that irked his cousin already.

"Mind if I join you?" A cheerful voice pulled him from his thoughts.

Rich squinted as he looked up, straight into two bright green pools of lust. He cocked an eyebrow in invitation to the stranger, whom he had seen earlier.

"Dan Robertson," the guy said with a grin as he sat next to him, holding out his hand.

"Rich Buchanan." Rich shook his hand. Dan's hand was softer than his own.

"So you're Frank's son?" Dan raised his eyebrows.

"Yes, sir, I am. And you are...?"

"Friend of the groom. I know all about the Buchanans though. Your family owns about half this county and practically the whole of Moone." Dan whistled, obviously impressed.

"Yes, we do. I've got the Moone part. Uncle Ted and Uncle Patrick have Reedlake." Rich couldn't help feeling smug.

"Yeah, I heard that." Dan nodded.

"You a wrangler?" Rich was intrigued. This guy had done his homework.

"Sure am. I work over at Tall Trees. D'you know it?"

Rich sniggered. "I know every ranch in Moone and Reedlake and quite a few beyond," he told him. "Tall Trees is Raymond Maddox's place out toward the east."

"You *do* know your stuff." Dan smiled.

Rich took another swig of his rum and leaned back on his elbows, looking at the lake. The sun was beginning to set, throwing a pinkish hue all around the ranch, glistening off the lake like tiny diamonds.

Dan leaned back too, idly running his finger over Rich's hand. Rich sighed. This guy sure was handsome and was obviously interested in him. He sat up after a few minutes, looking around them. The speeches must have finished as there were lots more people milling around outside now.

"You wanna go somewhere?" His heart thumped loudly as he gazed into Dan's brilliant green eyes.

Dan nodded and followed him around to the other side of the lake. There was a small copse which was quite shaded, offering them privacy and darkness.

Once they were far enough into the middle of the woodland, Rich pinned his partner to a large oak tree and devoured his mouth while unbuckling the guy's belt. Dan's lips were thin and he willingly allowed Rich's tongue to delve into the depths of his mouth.

Rich felt Dan's fingers on his zipper and Dan soon had his heaving cock in his hand, tugging eagerly.

Dan's cock sprang free and Rich pumped it hard. Dan groaned, throwing his head back against the tree. Rich saw him arch his back, thrusting his cock hard into Rich's large, calloused hand. He obligingly tugged at Dan's hard cock, eliciting a surge of thick juice which trailed lazily over his hand.

"Turn around," Rich growled, letting go of Dan's dick.

Dan turned to face the tree trunk and Rich yanked down the guy's pants. Dan grabbed his own cock and continued the rhythm Rich had started. Rich kicked Dan's legs farther apart and primed his lily-white ass while pumping his own heaving erection. Whipping a condom from his pocket, Rich sheathed himself before thrusting hard into the guy's waiting hole.

"Fuck!" Dan cursed as Rich's massive cock impaled him, stretching his tight rim, barging its way through his ass like a red-hot poker. Rich hissed at the tightness, giving them both a moment to adjust, before beginning his rough assailment on his partner. Rich held onto Dan's hips, pounding him hard over and over.

"Ahh... I'm gonna blow!" Dan howled, jerking his own dick like mad.

"Me too, brother," Rich gasped.

There was a loud groan from Dan as his dick exploded over his hand and dripped down the tree trunk. Rich grunted as he shot his seed, hammering into his partner over and over again until they both fell on the bracken, panting hard.

Rich found Dan's mouth and his tongue lapped at his lips before plunging into his hot, wet cavity. He closed his eyes as he held the guy in his arms, his hands trailing through his straight, sandy-colored hair. He could feel Dan's moans reverberating through his chest.

"Our little secret, OK, friend?" Rich grabbed a

handful of notes from the pocket of his pants and handed them to Dan, who gawked in surprise.

Suddenly a bright flash pulled them from their reverie. Rich leaped to his feet and stared into the shadows.

"Well, well. Just as I always thought." Joey's face sneered at them triumphantly as he clutched his camera.

Love or money—which would you choose?

For a couple of pretty girls like Danni and Alice, getting laid by ten different guys in ten nights should be a lot of fun. Especially with the promise of £1,000 just for telling Ray Morville, the owner of the local bar, all about it. But when Danni still has two guys to go and it's already day nine, she decides she's had enough.

What started as a fun competition on a drunken night out—as well as the end to her pressing financial worries —has ended with her feeling exhausted, regretful and desperate.

So, when her car breaks down and she's rescued by a couple of gorgeous hunks who teach her the delights of ménage romance, she should thank her lucky stars that her worries are finally over, right?

Except that Danni has already developed feelings for the handsome guys. Is it the end of her financial worries or the start of something much bigger?

~May I ask a Favor?~

I really hope you enjoyed Ménage on Moone Mountain and, if so, I'd be more than grateful if you'd leave me a review at any or all of the following sites. A review only has to be one or two words, saying what you thought of the book, or a more in-depth summary of what you liked or disliked about it.

Reviews help other readers find books and your opinion could help the author sell the book.

Reviews can be left at:

https://www.goodreads.com/author/show/7558233.Bella_Settarra

https://www.bookbub.com/authors/bella-settarra

Or any other blogs/review sites.

Thank you so much 😊

The Men of Moone Mountain Series

Ménage on Moone Mountain (Book One)
Red-Light Wrangler (Book Two)
Ménage on Ryder Ranch (Book Three)
Ménage at the Mode Boutique (Book Four)

The Cowboys of Cavern County Series

Carla's Cowboys (Book One)
Maggie's Man (Book Two)
Two for Trinity (Book Three)
Isla's Irish Cowboy (Book Four)
Savannah's Saviors (Book Five)
Rihanna's Rancher (Book Six)

The *Collar and Cuffs* Series

Waiting on Summer (Book One)
Waiting on Tuesday (Book Two)
Waiting on April (Book Three)
Waiting on Dawn (Book Four)
Waiting on Heaven (Book Five)
Waiting on Hope (Book Six)
Waiting on the Dom (Book Seven)

Standalone Novellas
Ménage and Mascara
Sex Mechanic
No Contest

The Collar & Cuffs Series

Light BDSM, Heavy on Romance

This seven-book series centres on the staff working in a salubrious Miami restaurant with a secret basement housing a well-equipped dungeon. Fancy a bite?

Reader discretion: series contains light BDSM, whipping, and spanking elements

Waiting On Summer

Collar & Cuffs Book One

He can dominate her body, but he can't control her past...

Summer Marsden hopes to have found safety and security working at the restaurant of Collar and Cuffs, a

salubrious club in a Miami. If she can just keep her head down and work hard, she will be able to cover the cost of her rent and bills, as well as put something toward the mounting debt accrued by her junkie ex-boyfriend.

Unexpectedly, she also finds love in the arms of Nathan Faulkener, one of the Doms who works at the club.

Nathan falls for Summer as soon as he meets her, and goes on to help her out of a sticky work situation. His affections for her continue to grow, and they begin a loving and steamy relationship in the dungeon of Collar and Cuffs. He is sure she feels the same way about him, although his instincts tell him she is in some kind of trouble.

Trouble has a name, Colin Cromer, and he is in deep shit. Since his cash cow, namely Summer Marsden, escaped his clutches, he has been drowning in debt—and drug-dealers can be deadly debtors. His only option is to find Summer and make her pay – in more ways than one.

Is Collar and Cuffs really as safe as Summer hopes? Or is her miserable past about to rob her of a happy future?

Buy Link: https://www.amazon.com/Carlas-Cowboys-Bella-Settarra/dp/1786860112

Her secrets may be well-hidden, but she can't hide her heart...

While on the run from Jerome Pearson, her dangerous boyfriend, Carla Burchfield falls in love with hunky twin cowboys, Matt and Dyson Shearer.

When Pearson turns up in town Carla's first instinct is to flee. Reluctantly leaving the guys, she makes her escape, only to be met with an accident en route. Local rancher, Aiden Fielding finds her and takes her back to his palatial spread, where he calls the doctor and the sheriff's office. To Carla's horror she discovers that the local Deputy Sheriff is, in fact, Dyson Shearer.

Feeling upset and betrayed she flees the ranch, taking with her a broken heart and a head full of secrets the guys would never believe.

When Pearson catches up with her, so does her past. Can she ever convince her cowboys that her reasons for hiding the stolen cash from a shop-raid are actually honorable? And can they persuade her to stay with them even though the affluent Aiden Fielding appears to have so much more to offer her?

In Bella's world all the heroes are gorgeous hunks and the heroines are always beautiful. Having said that, she firmly believes that 'handsome is as handsome does' and that 'beauty is in the eye of the beholder'. (She is also a big fan of clichés as well as alliteration!)

She has been hanging out with her 'imaginary friends' for several years now and finds the profession exhilarating and intriguing. Her stories are all Steamy Romances, although they vary considerably in subject-matter.

She loves writing Cowboy Romances and was thrilled when the first book in her *The Men of Moone Mountain* series, entitled *Ménage on Moone Mountain,* received a nomination for the **Ménage Romances Fan's Award 2015** and became an **ARe Bestseller**, and the third book in this series, *Ménage on Ryder Ranch* was also nominated for the **Erotic Ménages Romances Award 2016**. As you can see, this series is now being re-released with new covers and published under Bella's own brand, Bella Settarra Publishing. This will enable the series to be available in Kindle Unlimited as well as in print version, and to have more special offers than before. There are also plans to extend the series beyond the original first four books. Watch this space...

Bella has also written other Cowboy series, one of which, *Midnight in Montana* (Siren Publishing), is currently a duo but she is considering expanding the series in the future. At the time of writing she has recently finished writing book six, *Rihanna's Rancher*, in her other cowboy series *The Cowboys of Cavern County* (Totally Bound Publishing)

Her *Collar and Cuffs* series also received an **ARe Bestseller Award** for *Waiting on Summer*. This series was set in a BDSM club in Miami, and was another joy to write. This series has also been revamped by Bella Settarra Publishing and at the time of writing is available in Kindle Unlimited, as well as to buy from Amazon.

She has also had several short stories and poems released in charity anthologies, and a few released under Bella Settarra Publishing; *No Contest*, (which is **free** with subscription to Bella's newsletter here), *Ménage and Mascara*, and *Sex Mechanic*.

Not everyone is perfect - but it's the character's flaws

that make them interesting, she believes. As in life, things don't always run smoothly, but it's the twists and turns which provide the drive to keep going, even when it just feels like an uphill struggle. Bella is currently fighting her own battle against breast cancer - a battle which she is determined to win - and believes that all women have the right to feel sexy even when they are battle-scarred.

She hopes you enjoy your foray into her world and would love to connect with you at: http://bellasettarrapublishing.com

Facebook: http://www.facebook.com/bella.settarra
Facebook: http://facebook.com/bpages/BellaSettarra
Twitter: http://twitter.com/BellaSettarra
Email: bellasettarra@gmail.com
Blog: http://bellasettarrabooks.blogspot.co.uk/

www.ingramcontent.com/pod-product-compliance
Lightning Source LLC
Chambersburg PA
CBHW070439170726
48291CB00002B/577